Aurora and Socrates

Aurora
and Socrates

Anne-Cath. Vestly

Translated from the Norwegian by Eileen Amos

Illustrated by Leonard Kessler

Thomas Y. Crowell Company
New York

First United States publication 1977
Copyright © 1969 by Tiden Norsk Forlag
English translation copyright © 1975 by Kestrel Books
Illustrations copyright © 1977 by
Thomas Y. Crowell Company, Inc.

Library of Congress Cataloging in Publication Data
Vestly, Anne-Cath. Aurora and Socrates.
Translation of Aurora og Sokrates.
SUMMARY: While their parents are working full time,
Aurora and her little brother Socrates cope with their
babysitters. [1. Family life—Fiction.
2. Baby sitters—Fiction. 3. Mothers—Employment—Fiction]
I. Kessler, Leonard P. II. Title.
PZ7.V6154Au [Fic] 76-43038 ISBN 0-690-01293-4
1 2 3 4 5 6 7 8 9 10

Contents

1. Father Finds a Way 6
2. Gran Comes to Building Z 21
3. Bala 36
4. A Funny Feeling 51
5. "Little Girl in Closet" 65
6. Something to Hang on the Wall 80
7. "We're Not Cows!" 91
8. Whispering through the Mailbox 103
9. "Wish Me Luck!" 116
10. Surprise, Surprise! 125
11. All Together Again 135

1 · Father Finds a Way

Aurora sat on a red sled in the middle of the living room on the tenth floor of Building Z at Tiriltoppen. She lived there with Mother, Father, and her little brother Socrates.

Tiriltoppen is just outside the big town and is almost a little town in itself. It has many apartment houses and shops, but the very best thing about it is the forest that lies behind the high buildings. If you take the path through the forest, you come to a little house that stands by itself. Beside it is a woodshed, a cowshed, and a tiny outhouse. In the cowshed live Rosie and Little Bull and five hens. In the house live Maren and Martin and Marte and Mads and Mona and Milly and Mina and Morten, who used to be called Little Morten, but isn't any longer because now he goes to school, their mother and father

6

and their grandmother. Aurora calls their grandmother
Gran, as the family does. Gran is Aurora's special friend.

The red sled had been a Christmas present from
Aurora's real Granny who lived in a town called Bessby.
It was the nicest present Aurora ever had, and she played
with it indoors as well as out of doors.

"Isn't it amazing how everything happens at once?"
said Father. "Today I had one letter from the university

telling me when I have to defend my thesis, and another letter from the university saying they would like me to give some lectures on ancient history. The man who was to give them has to be away for six months. They asked me to replace him. It will mean extra work for me, but I'm very pleased they want me."

"Have you learned enough in school to be able to teach now?" asked Aurora.

"I hope I'll always be learning more and more, but I know enough to do this job. I'll be able to lecture with a clear conscience, and I'll earn some money, too."

"Yes," said Mother, looking very thoughtful.

"Well?" said Father. "What is it?"

"I'm only wondering what we'll do here," said Mother.

"Maybe you'll stay at home?" said Aurora.

"I?" said Mother. "Is that what *you* think, Edward? It's taken me years to learn my job. I don't want to give it all up now."

"I'll arrange something," said Father. "There are plenty of kindergartens and day nurseries. Up to now I could take care of Aurora and Socrates and study too, but maybe we could make a few inquiries."

"I can play outside until you come home, Daddy," said Aurora, "and I can baby-sit for Socrates, too."

"No, that won't do," said Father. "I'll be gone for hours, you know. You'd have to bring Socrates in and change him, and if he has a cold he can't go outside at all. But don't worry. I'll arrange everything tomorrow."

He sounded as though it were the easiest thing in the world, and so Aurora didn't worry, but that evening, when Mother and Father thought she was asleep, she heard them talking. At first their voices sounded just as usual, but suddenly Mother's rose higher and Father's became sharper. Aurora lay there wide awake. At last they were speaking so loudly that she couldn't help hearing everything they said.

"Do you really want Aurora to hang around here waiting for us?" said Mother. "That's just what I've been afraid of."

"I know," said Father, "but you seriously don't expect me to turn down a job at the university, do you?"

"No, of course not," said Mother. "Obviously I'm the one who has to stay home now because I've had a job for several years. But it's just beginning to get interesting at work."

"I'm not saying that you have to stop," said Father hotly. "I'll arrange something and the children won't suffer. That's the most important thing. We'll find a solution that is right for all of us, but you needn't look like that just because I want to do something more than wash diapers!"

"All right," said Mother. "I won't say another word."

And she didn't. There was no further sound, and Aurora thought that this was even worse. Angry words

seemed to be drifting around the apartment. They hung in the air and made it difficult to breathe. At last Aurora fell asleep, but when she woke up the next morning she wasn't happy. She had such a bad feeling inside as if she was afraid of something. She wondered if Mother was keeping her word and still not saying anything. She was, in a funny kind of way, because she spoke quite naturally to Aurora and Socrates, but she didn't say anything at all to Father and had a distant look in her eyes. She packed her own lunch and was in a great hurry to leave. Father was busy making the beds when she went, so he didn't say good-bye either.

Aurora went in to see Socrates. At least he was his usual self. Or was he a little different?

He seemed to know that Aurora was unhappy. He kept patting her on the head and saying, "Soc'ates loves Auwowa, nice to Auwowa."

"Mommy and Daddy aren't friends, Socrates," said Aurora, "and it's our fault. If they didn't have us they would be friends and go into town together and do a lot of work and earn some money. And Daddy wouldn't have washed diapers, but he hardly washes any now because you're such a good boy except when we've been out with you too long or you lose your temper, otherwise you're all right. . . . Do you remember the story of Hansel and Gretel, Socrates?"

"Mmmm," said Socrates, and hugged her as hard as he could.

"It was like this," said Aurora. "They didn't have enough to eat, and their mother sent them into the forest and told them to stay there because there wasn't any food for them at home. . . ."

Now Aurora knew very well it wasn't like this at her house, but she was feeling miserable. When she began to think about the story it seemed sad yet thrilling at the same time. When Father asked her if she would take care of Socrates out of doors for a little while until he came and joined them, she said yes at once, and hurried to get ready. Father dressed Socrates. "Shall I put him in his fur sleeping-bag in the baby carriage?" he asked.

"No, we'll play with the sled," said Aurora.

"All right," said Father. He put Socrates into an extra pair of woolly pants and wrapped a thick scarf around his neck. Finally Socrates looked like a little ball that could barely roll along, but he and Aurora and the red sled got downstairs somehow.

Aurora knew exactly what she would do. She would go along the path through the forest, just like Hansel and Gretel. They would go on and on and on, and Mommy and Daddy would be sorry because they didn't have Aurora and Socrates any more.

Aurora put Socrates on the sled. She wanted to get out of sight before Father came down, but Socrates kept falling off, so that she had to go slowly.

"You can lie on the sled and look at the ground," said Aurora, and for once Socrates did what she told him. He thought it was fun to see the ground passing quickly beneath him.

When they had gone a little way, they met a small boy. It was Morten, one of the children from the house in the woods. He knew Aurora and she knew him, but neither of them spoke, Aurora because she was running away from home and Morten because he was so shy that he wouldn't be the first one to say hello when he ran into a little girl unexpectedly. And so they just passed each other and said nothing.

When Morten was out of sight, Aurora thought she had gone a long way. Socrates didn't want to lay on the sled any longer. He wanted to walk, and that made them slow. He would walk a little way, and then turn around to pick up a lump of snow lying on the path. Then he wanted to push the sled, but he just made it go crooked.

"You're very hard to run away with," said Aurora. Still, she couldn't see her apartment building any more, not even if she stood on tiptoe. There were just trees everywhere.

"Get on the sled, Socrates," she said, for suddenly it was very quiet in the forest.

She went on and on. By now Daddy must know that she had gone. She looked around at Socrates and found that he had taken off one of his woollen mittens. It was nowhere to be seen, and his little hand was red and cold.

"Socrates," said Aurora, "you don't do things like that. Here, you can have mine." Her glove was nice and dry, and his had been wet and cold, so Socrates was delighted with the exchange. Aurora put one hand in her pocket and pulled the sled with the other, but it wasn't easy. Socrates was little, but he was heavy. She had to drag the sleeve of her sweater down over her hand so that she could pull with both hands again.

When she had been walking for some time, she caught sight of the house in the woods. If only Gran were at home, maybe she could go in and warm herself for a little while before she went any farther.

Aurora approached the house cautiously. Was anyone home? Smoke was rising from the chimney and she could hear a dog barking its head off. That was Stovepipe—and shortly afterward Gran came out.

"Why, are you little people out for a walk?" she said.
"Come in, come in. I suppose your father isn't far behind
you?"

"Oh yes he is," said Aurora. "He doesn't know we're
here because we've run away."

"My goodness!" said Gran, looking at Aurora. "Have
you and Socrates run away? You'd better stay here, then,
because I'm all alone. Every one of the children is at
school and their mother has gone to town today."

Gran put Socrates on her lap and warmed him and
took off one of his sweaters. Socrates looked happy as
he sat there waving to Stovepipe. He seemed to think
that running away was fun, and Aurora felt it wasn't so
bad either—only she couldn't stop thinking about how
sad Daddy would be not to see them any more.

Socrates was given Morten's old bricks to play with, and Gran started to make some waffles. Aurora talked to Stovepipe and watched Gran.

"You don't have a phone at home, do you?" said Gran.

"No," said Aurora.

"I don't know what to do," said Gran. "I can't leave the house because Rosie is going to calve and I don't want her to be alone."

Aurora understood that. When they had eaten their waffles, Marte came in from school. Gran said, "I wonder if you could be a good girl and take Aurora and Socrates home. Don't leave them until you've made sure someone's there."

"All right," said Marte. She was tall and blonde and looked kind. Aurora knew at once that she wouldn't be afraid to go with her. Gran gave them a thick rug to wrap around Socrates on the sled.

Marte didn't have to go very far. In a little while, they met Father.

Father had played detective. He had been to the supermarket and all around Tiriltoppen. At last he had gone back to Building Z and asked all the children playing there if they had seen Aurora and Socrates. Finally he had found sled tracks heading toward the woods. When he had walked a little way he had found a woollen

mitten, the one that belonged to Socrates. That made Father very happy, but when he met them he was angry. At any rate his voice sounded quite gruff to Aurora.

"Where have you been?" he said.

"We thought we'd go into the forest and never come back," said Aurora, "but Gran said you'd be worried about us and so Marte was bringing us home."

"Thank you very much, Marte," said Father, "and thank Gran for me."

"Gran couldn't come because Rosie is going to have a calf soon," said Aurora.

"Is that so?" said Father. "I hope you'll let us know when it's born, Marte. We'd like to come and see it."

"Of course," said Marte. She turned and went back home. Father said, "How could you frighten me so, Aurora?"

But Aurora couldn't explain all that had been in her mind. She just held Father's hand. In her head she said that Mommy and Daddy were fighting and maybe they would be friends again if she and Socrates went to live in the woods.

But she didn't say anything out loud. All the same, Daddy seemed to understand something of what she had been saying to herself.

"Mommy and I will find a way," he said. "Don't worry, Aurora. Now we'll go to the day nursery and talk to the woman who runs it."

At the nursery, a lot of children were playing outside. More of them were inside making things with clay, and four of them were doing carpentry.

"You and Socrates could learn a lot here," said Father. But when they spoke to the lady in charge, she looked sorry and said, "I would be glad to have them, but I haven't room. There's a long waiting list, and we have to take people in turn."

"I understand," said Father. "What about next year?"

"I don't know yet," said the lady, "and I can't promise anything."

"Oh well," said Father, "there's nothing you can do for us then."

He went out again and walked on, thinking hard.

"Are you feeling miserable?" asked Aurora.

"Oh, it's not so bad," said Father. "As long as you don't run away again we'll be all right."

"We were pretending to be Hansel and Gretel," said Aurora, "but we didn't come to a witch's house, we came to Gran's, and we had waffles."

"Yes," said Father. "I wonder whether. . . . No, it wouldn't do. . . ."

When Mother came home she was her usual self and spoke cheerfully to all of them, even Father.

She and Father didn't have a serious talk until they were quite sure that Aurora was asleep.

"How many times a week will you have to go to the university?" asked Mother.

"Three days," said Father.

"We need to get regular help, then," said Mother.

"We don't need help every day," said Father. "I can do a lot on the days when I don't go out."

"We must find someone the children like," said Mother.

"Give me one more day, and we'll see," said Father.

"I've got the day off from the office tomorrow," said Mother, "so I'll be at home."

The next day Father went off to town early in the morning, and Mother stayed at home. Aurora helped her with all the work so the apartment looked just as nice as

19

it did when Father was there. He was away a very long time. When at last he came back he just changed into his heavy walking shoes and went out again.

He came home for dinner and said, "I think we've fixed it. Uncle Brande will come two days every week and Gran will come on the third. Or rather, if it's a nice day, the children will go to Gran's and stay there until we come and get them. Uncle Brande was pleased at the idea of earning some extra money, but he can only work two days."

"Yes," said Mother, "but couldn't Gran come all three days?"

"No, she's too busy," said Father, smiling. "She has to go to town twice a week for something special she's doing, and then she has her animals to look after, you know."

"Mmm," said Mother. "It's good that both of them know the children."

"Yes," said Father, "it will only be until the summer and then we'll see what we can think of for next year."

"We'll take one year at a time," said Mother.

"Yes," said Father, lifting her off her feet.

"Socrates and I won't need to run away any more, then," said Aurora.

2 · Gran Comes to Building Z

Today was Tuesday, but at Aurora's house they didn't
call it Tuesday any more, they called it Gransday. On the
first Gransday everything went smoothly. The weather
was fine, and Father pulled Aurora and Socrates on the
sled over to the house in the woods before he went to
town. Socrates played in the yard, and Aurora went to
see Rosie's little calf. But she had to promise Gran that
she would talk to Little Bull as well. "He's used to being
the only calf," said Gran. "It's not so easy for him to
have a little sister all of a sudden."

Little Bull had grown even bigger since she last saw
him, thought Aurora, but Gran said he was just like a
little child, and Gran knew about animals, so she had to
believe her. Aurora was allowed to feed the hens, too.
Then she played with Stovepipe. Now that Morten went

to school, Stovepipe found the house very quiet in the daytime.

The next time it was Gransday, Socrates had a cold and Father went to the red telephone box at Tiriltoppen and called up the house in the woods. He explained that Socrates couldn't go out.

"I'll come over," said Gran into the telephone.

"Fine," said Father. "I don't have to leave for a few minutes, so if you can get here soon, we'll have a minute to talk before I go."

Yes, Gran said, she would be right there. She got ready and started off.

"It's not bad, going out to work again," she said to herself. To be sure, she did a lot of work at home for

her daughter, her son-in-law, and the eight children, who were her grandchildren, but she hadn't gone out to work since she was a dairy maid, and that was a long time ago. She was in high spirits. She knew every tree along the way, but when she came out of the woods, passed the supermarket, and approached the apartments, she didn't feel quite so cheerful.

"Well," she said to herself, "there's nothing to be afraid of." She walked up to Building Z as quickly as she could. But when she got inside, she stopped. There was the elevator, and over there were the stairs. Aurora and Socrates lived on the tenth floor. Gran was active enough, but she wasn't supposed to climb so many stairs at her age. She wasn't used to elevators, though. In fact, she had never been in one before. She looked at the elevator door for a long time. People were coming out of it now. There must be a lot of folks leaving the apartments at this hour. If only somebody would come along who wanted to go *in*. Aurora's father would be on the lookout for her. If only she had said that she would wait down here. But she hadn't thought about the elevator when she spoke over the phone.

Gran went up to the elevator door several times. Once she got as far as opening it, but she didn't dare go in. Supposing it started off before both her legs were inside? Gran took a long step backward, something went click inside the elevator, and it shot up without her.

23

Soon it came down again full of people who were going to work. The elevator went up again. Gran stood there. At last a woman came in through the front door. She went straight up to the elevator and pushed the button impatiently.

"Is it hard to get the elevator today?" she asked. "I'm late."

"No, it's been up and down several times," said Gran.

"Ah," said the lady, "here it comes. Please go in first, you've been waiting."

"Oh no," said Gran, "I can't. . . ."

"Oh I see," said the lady, and pushed her gently in. She followed her and said, "Which floor?"

"The tenth," said Gran, "but it doesn't matter. I'll get out and you can go on your own."

"No, that's all right," said the woman, "I want the eighth floor." She pushed the button with the number eight on it, and the elevator began to move. Gran stood in a corner with her face to the wall and covered her eyes with her hands.

"You're not sick, are you?" asked the lady.

"Oh no," said Gran, shaking her head, "but I'm not used to going in an elevator."

"It's easy," said the lady. "You just push the right button. If you want the tenth floor, push number ten."

The elevator stopped, and the woman got out at the eighth floor. Gran was alone once more. She didn't dare to move. If she walked across the elevator to reach the buttons, it might drop to the ground floor again. Now it was on the eighth floor. That was a long way to fall. Oh dear, what had she gotten herself mixed up in? Gran stayed in her corner. She had not been there very long when a man and a woman opened the elevator door. They nodded to Gran, pushed a button, and the elevator went down.

"Just as I thought," said Gran to herself. "Now we're going to fall."

But no, the elevator went down nice and smoothly,

and there they were on the ground floor again. Gran stayed where she was. It seemed as if her legs wouldn't move. They wouldn't walk out of the elevator, although that was the only thing she wanted to do at this moment.

But the woman who had come down in the elevator with her thought it was strange that Gran didn't get out. She got back in the elevator. "Is everything all right?"

"No," said Gran. "I'm afraid to work the elevator. The doctor said I shouldn't climb stairs and I've got to get to the tenth floor."

"I'll go up with you," said the woman. "Just go on," she said to her husband. "I'll catch up."

She took Gran right up to the tenth floor, and Gran shook hands with her and thanked her warmly. "That was very kind of you," she said.

Then she went out of the elevator. Aurora was watching in the long hall because her father had told her to look out for Gran who might not know which door to come to.

"Here I am," said Aurora.

Father was waiting with his hat and coat on. "Splendid, Gran," he said. "Aurora knows where the cough medicine is if Socrates needs it. If there's anything else, just ask her."

When Father had gone, Gran flopped down on a kitchen stool. "You're not sick are you?" asked Aurora.

"Oh no," said Gran, "but I've been scared out of my wits."

"Was someone rude to you?" asked Aurora in alarm.

"No," said Gran, "but I've never been in an elevator before."

"Were you frightened?" asked Aurora. "It helps if you go up and down lots of times. I did that, and now I don't mind going in it by myself."

"Do you really think it helps?" said Gran.

"Yes," said Aurora. That morning, when Socrates was asleep, the elevator in Building Z had a busy time. It went up and down for a whole hour. Aurora and Gran were inside it, and neither of them stood in a corner with her face to the wall. At last Aurora said, "Try it on your own, Gran."

"Oh I can't," said Gran.

"Yes you can," said Aurora. "You can come and pick me up on the fifth floor."

So Gran stood in the elevator by herself again. For a minute she was as scared as she had been earlier in the day. She wanted to hide in the corner, but she pulled herself together and pushed the button. First she went down to the ground floor. Then she went up to the fifth and got Aurora.

"You did it," said Aurora. "You are okay."

When they got back to the tenth floor, some people were waiting for the elevator. "It's lucky you came," they

27

said, "or we would be stuck. We've been pushing and pushing the button.

"Well I never!" said Gran. "Where do you want to go?"

"We're going down."

"I'll take you," said Gran.

They looked surprised, but they didn't say anything. Gran stood there like a sergeant and pushed buttons for all she was worth.

"Thank you," they said when they reached the ground floor.

"You're welcome," said Gran, and whizzed up to the tenth floor again.

"We have to go and get Socrates," said Aurora.

"Yes, we must," said Gran with a sigh. At that moment she would rather have had a job as an elevator operator than as a nursemaid, but it couldn't be helped.

"You'll have to take your boots off," said Aurora when they went in.

"This floor isn't made for heavy boots, is it?" said Gran.

"No, they make a clumping noise on the ceiling of the people downstairs," said Aurora. "Did you bring slippers?"

"No, but I can walk around in my stockinged feet." She took off her boots, put them in the bathroom, trotted around in her thick gray stockings, and nobody could hear that she was there. But the boots weren't the only things she had to take off. Gran was well wrapped up. At home, in the house in the woods, it was drafty because it was an old wooden house. Gran was used to wearing two knitted sweaters indoors, but it was much too warm for that here. Building Z had central heating.

Even after she had taken off one sweater, she had to go to the balcony door and stick her head out.

"Are you looking for something, Gran?" asked Aurora.

"No," said Gran, "only I can't breathe in here." She wasn't used to the warm, dry air of Building Z, but she would be all right if she got a few breaths of fresh air outside the door now and then. There was another reason, too, why she wanted to go out on the balcony.

29

She had never been up on the tenth floor, and it might be fun to look down. The first time she just looked straight out in front of her, and the second time she took a little peep at the fir tree which looked so tiny from up above.

"Oh, you old silly!" said Gran to herself.

She hurried indoors, and it was some time before she went out again. Then she stood for a little while and closed her eyes and leaned cautiously over the edge of the balcony. "I think I'll risk it," she said. She opened her eyes a little way and looked down. Suddenly, she felt she wanted to let go and fall down and down until she landed on the ground.

"Ugh!" said Gran and went indoors again.

"Are you okay?" asked Aurora.

"I feel as if I might jump even though I don't want to," said Gran.

"Don't go out there, then," said Aurora. "If you want fresh air, you'd better go into my bedroom and open the window."

Usually, Socrates slept in Aurora's room, but since he was sick he was in with Father and Mother so if he cried they could hear. Now he was sitting up in his bed, calling out, "Soc'ates' thirsty."

Gran went into the kitchen to get some orange juice, but the floor here was much slipperier than the one at home, and she was in her stockinged feet. Before she knew what was happening, she fell flat on her back.

Gran was wearing two thick skirts, so that she hardly hurt herself at all. "No bones broken," she said, and after that she walked more carefully, especially going around corners.

"May I go out for a while?" asked Aurora. "I'd like to play with my sled."

"You go ahead, my dear," said Gran. "I'll take care of Socrates."

"If I meet Nusse and Brit-Karen, may I bring them to see you?" asked Aurora.

"Of course," said Gran.

Gran had a little chat with Socrates and went back into the living room. There was something she wanted

31

to try. She had thought about it ever since she had come into the room. It was the piano. There was no piano in the house in the woods. She looked at it for a long time. The lid was open, and the keys seemed to be waiting for her. She put her finger on one and pressed it so gently that it made no sound.

"Hm," said Gran, "that wasn't much good." It looked so easy when somebody sat and played with both hands. Their fingers seemed to move of their own accord. She put both hands on the keys, and there were a lot of sounds at once.

A little boy stood in the doorway. Socrates had climbed out of bed. "Soc'ates p'ay," he said.

"All right," said Gran, "you and I together. That's what's called a duet."

She put Socrates on her lap. There was nothing cautious about *him*. He made a dive at the keys, and that made Gran much bolder. The piano had never produced so many sounds at once. Socrates sang as well, and Gran hummed. They were both enjoying themselves and were absorbed in what they were doing. They didn't notice the knocking on the wall. The ringing at the door had happened once, twice, and three times before they came to a stop and heard the bell.

"A body can't play in peace here," said Gran. At home in the house in the woods, she didn't mind visitors, but here she wondered whether she should open the door or not. She didn't know who was outside.

"Shall I open the door?" she asked Socrates.

"P'ay again," said Socrates, and flung himself at the keys.

Gran got up and took Socrates with her. "You go back in bed," she said, "I'll get a banana for you, and then I'll find out who's ringing the bell."

She crept into the hall. "What on earth is going on? Isn't anyone at home?" she heard a voice say. "Are the children alone, I wonder? It wouldn't surprise me."

There was another ring, a loud one, but Gran went back to Socrates without making a sound. She gave him the banana and sat down and looked at a book with lovely pictures in it.

The bell rang several times, but Gran didn't open the door. The person who was standing outside didn't sound friendly.

She didn't dare to play the piano any more, so she just sat in Socrates's room and talked to him. A little later on, the bell rang again, but now she wasn't afraid to open the door because Aurora called "Gran!" through the mail slot.

Three little girls stood outside, Nusse and Brit-Karen and Aurora.

"Now you can see for yourselves," said Aurora. "It's quite true about Gran." Nusse and Brit-Karen stared at Gran, and Gran nodded and said, "Yes, it's true."

"We're going to get dinner now," said Aurora, "so you two can't stay."

When Father came home, Gran told him, "Socrates and I played together today, and somebody came and rang the bell, but I didn't open the door."

"Yes, I know," said Father. "I've had a talk with the people who live in the apartment downstairs—they were on the lookout for me when I got into the elevator. I'll tell you something, Gran. When I play, I put a rug over the piano and some towels here under the lid. Then the noise isn't so loud."

Gran hid her face in her hands and looked ashamed, but Father patted her cheek and said, "Of course you can play again, Gran, now you know the trick with the rug and the towels. Apart from that, how did you like living in an apartment?"

"Your floors are very slippery," said Gran, "and at first I couldn't breathe, but I'm used to the hot air now."

"I'm sure Socrates will be better next Tuesday," said Father, "so you won't have to come here."

"She learned how to work the elevator," said Aurora, "so she won't mind coming again."

"I didn't know you hadn't done that before," said Father.

"A body's never too old to learn," said Gran. Then she went home. That evening, everybody in the house in the woods heard what it was like to live in Building Z.

3 · Bala

Today was Daddy's day. Aurora knew this the moment she woke up. The day Gran came was a cozy sort of day, and the days when Uncle Brande was there were exciting, but the days when Daddy was at home were the best of all. She made a doghouse for Little Puff under her quilt. She pretended to be a dog too, because it was fun to sit inside the quilt doghouse. She played this game for such a long time that Father came in to wake her.

"Aurora," he said cautiously.

"Woof woof," said Aurora.

"Help!" said Father. "Marie, there's a dog in here. You've always wanted one, haven't you?"

Although Mother wasn't yet quite awake, she came in and peered at the quilt doghouse.

"Woof woof," said Aurora again. Mother peeped under the quilt.

"Isn't this a lovely doghouse?" said Aurora.

"Yes," said Mother. "I wish you could go to the office instead of me today, Aurora, and I could stay at home with Daddy."

"Are you going to court today?" asked Aurora.

"Yes," said Mother. "A boy has been stealing cars. What do you think we should do with him?"

"Is he nice or mean?" asked Aurora.

"He's human," said Mother, "so he's a little of both, like the rest of us."

"Tell him to work and earn some money, so he can buy his own car," said Aurora. "He can buy a used one."

"What sort of work would he like?" asked Mother.

"Something with cars," said Aurora.

"Marie," said Father firmly, "unless you get a move on, you'll be late. You can't stay in here talking to Aurora all morning."

When at last Mother was ready to go, Socrates looked anxiously at Father. He was afraid Father might go, too. He clung to one of Father's legs and held tight while Father was helping Mother on with her coat.

"Have a nice day, all of you," said Mother. "See you at dinnertime, Socrates."

"Dinnertime," said Socrates.

Father was in high spirits today. He whistled and sang while he did the housework. Socrates and Aurora helped him. As soon as Father had made the beds, Socrates crawled over the quilt to add a finishing touch. When Father brought the mop, Socrates took one of his shirts and dipped it in the bucket so that he could scrub the floor, too.

"Hm," said Father. "That's fine, Socrates. But instead of doing that, why don't you pick up the crumbs from the living room rug?"

Socrates started to work, but Father discovered that he was putting the crumbs into his mouth instead of into the dustpan.

"Put the crumbs here, Socrates," said Father.

"Yes," said Socrates. He found a tiny crumb and put it in the dustpan, and then into his mouth.

"I'll get him an apple," whispered Aurora.

"Look what Socrates has got," she said, handing him an apple.

"Yes," said Socrates. He put the apple into the dustpan and left it there.

"We'll let him help with the dishes," said Father. This was a great success. Socrates had a little bowl of warm soapy water all to himself. He washed two teaspoons and his own cup. Aurora wiped all the knives and forks, Father put the other things into a rack to dry, and that was that.

There was a ring at the door. Nusse's mother stood there. "Is your father studying?" she asked Aurora.

"No," said Aurora. "He's writing a shopping list. I'm going to the supermarket."

"Could I interrupt him for a minute or two?"

"I think so," said Aurora. "Here he is."

"The thing is, we got a piano for Christmas and a new vacuum cleaner, too," said Nusse's mother.

"Yes," said Father, looking confused. "How nice for you to have a piano." He didn't quite know what to say about the vacuum cleaner, but that didn't matter, for Nusse's mother went on: "Yes, we're buying both of them on credit. We can afford it because we've finished paying for the electric mixer and the deep-freeze. I've taken a part-time job in the supermarket to help out."

"That's splendid," said Father.

"So what I thought was this," said Nusse's mother, "and do tell me if you don't like the idea. I thought that if your Daddy would teach Nusse to play the piano he could have our vacuum cleaner, the old one of course, but it's just as good as the new one, only it isn't the latest model."

She said this to Aurora, but Father was listening. That was just what Nusse's mother wanted him to do. She wasn't shy about talking to Aurora.

"Well now," said Father.

"I never learned to play myself," said Nusse's mother. "It would be so nice if Nusse could have lessons—especially now that we've got a piano."

Father thought it over, and then he said, "Yes, I understand. We can work something out. I'm busy three days a week, but I could spare a little time on the other days. Say twice a week, half an hour each time?"

"Oh, that's wonderful," said Nusse's mother. "I'm so glad."

"I'll have to stop the lessons for a week or so before my exam," said Father.

"Of course," said Nusse's mother. "Will you be a doctor then?"

"Yes," said Father, "if everything goes well I'll have my Ph.D."

"I'll go and get the vacuum cleaner right now," said Nusse's mother. "I'm really sorry I've taken a job and can't help you with Socrates."

"Don't give it a thought," said Father.

Soon afterward, there was a ring at the door again and Nusse's mother stood there with the cleaner.

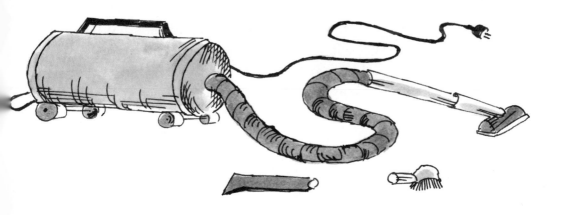

"Goodness me," said Father, "what a nice thing for us to be getting."

"Well, I have to go," said Nusse's mother. "I should have been at work by now. The cleaner is ready to use."

"Tell Nusse she can come at ten o'clock tomorrow morning," said Father.

"Thanks very much," shouted Nusse's mother. She was already a long way down the hall.

Father, Aurora, and Socrates were on their own with the vacuum cleaner.

"Shall we try it?" asked Father, looking at the living room rug which had had quite a lot of crumbs and other bits dropped on it recently.

"Oh yes!" said Aurora, hopping up and down.

Socrates hopped too, but kept his distance.

Father plugged in the vacuum, but nothing happened. Then he discovered the little button that had to be pushed in. There was a rushing and a roaring and a terrible droning noise. The vacuum lay on the floor. It seemed to be hissing to itself. Father took the handle firmly. He put it on the carpet, and the crumbs and bits of pieces almost flew into the hose. It was funny to watch. Father and Aurora tried to talk, but the vacuum cleaner made more noise than they did. At last Father gave the cleaner to Aurora so that she could try. "Where's Socrates?" he shouted in her ear.

Aurora shook her head and went on vacuuming.

Father looked in the bathroom and the bedroom and the kitchen and Aurora's room. No Socrates. He started to look again. He went back into the bedroom, knelt down, and looked under the bed. There lay Socrates.

"Bala," he shrieked. "It's Bala—boo hoo-oooo."

"No it isn't," said Father. He had no idea what Bala was, but he realized it must be something frightening.

"Come here, Socrates, I'll take care of you," he said.

"Bala take Soc'ates," said Socrates.

"Do you want Aurora to go to the supermarket and buy you an orange?" said Father.

"Owange," said Socrates, and crawled quick as lightning under the bed again.

Meanwhile Aurora was busy vacuuming. The rug looked beautiful. There wasn't a single crumb left. What should she clean now? There were no more rugs to do. She looked around.

On the end table were the earrings that Mommy wore when she got dressed up. Usually they were kept in a little box in the bedroom, but now they were in here. They were two gold earrings with a little pearl in each. They didn't look very shiny today, thought Aurora. Perhaps if she vacuumed them they would be much brighter. How pleased Mommy would be. She lifted the vacuum hose up to them and the earrings disappeared just like the crumbs. She heard them jingling down the hose before the cleaner swallowed them up. She was so frightened that she dropped the hose. Father came in and switched off the cleaner. "Socrates is scared of it. I think we'd better stop for a while and give him time to get used to it."

"Daddy," said Aurora.

"I really believe you're scared of it too," said Father, for Aurora looked thoroughly frightened.

"No," said Aurora, "but I . . ." She was going to tell about the earrings, but Socrates came in. He was still crying a little, but he managed to sob, "Auwowa owange." "Bala go away—no Bala," he said when he saw the vacuum. It wasn't making any noise now, so he didn't mind standing in the doorway for a minute. Then he turned and ran into the hall.

44

"Hi, Socrates!" said Father.

"Daddy," said Aurora.

"Yes," said Father, "I think I must go calm down Socrates. Put your things on, Aurora, and go to the supermarket and buy four oranges. They're not on the list. Do you think you can remember them?"

"Yes," said Aurora. It seemed just as if the earrings were disappearing further and further into the vacuum while Daddy was talking. She had better tell him later.

"I think Marie will get a surprise when she comes home today," said Father.

"Yes," said Aurora.

When she got to the supermarket, she asked for the oranges first so that she wouldn't forget them. One of the store assistants helped her to find all the other things on her list. When she was leaving the store, she caught sight of Brit-Karen and Nusse.

They didn't look their usual selves at all.

"We don't feel much like talking today," said Nusse, "but can we walk home with you?"

"Of course," said Aurora. She took a good look at them. Brit-Karen had a very woebegone expression, and Nusse seemed to be unhappy, too.

"What's the matter?" asked Aurora.

"It's something about Brit-Karen," said Nusse sadly.

"Oh," said Aurora. She tried to think of all the things that could make you miserable, but couldn't find one at the moment.

45

"Shall I tell her, Brit-Karen?" said Nusse, "or will you?"

"I'll tell her," said Brit-Karen, "because it's really about me—no, you tell her."

"Brit-Karen's going to move," said Nusse, "and we shall never see each other again."

"What?" said Aurora. "Oh, poor Brit-Karen!"

"Poor me, too," said Nusse. "Don't forget that Brit-Karen and I have been friends since we were little."

"Oh yes," said Aurora.

"You can come and be miserable with us," said Nusse.

"I'll just take these groceries upstairs first," said Aurora.

"We'll come with you," said Nusse.

Now there were three girls looking miserable. Father was alarmed when he opened the door and saw the three unhappy faces.

"What's the matter, Aurora?" he asked.

"Brit-Karen's going to move," said Aurora, "and we'll never see her again."

"Good gracious me!" said Father. "Where are you moving, Brit-Karen?"

"To that apartment building down there," said Brit-Karen, pointing.

"Oh well, that's not so far," said Father. Aurora, too, was surprised when she heard Brit-Karen's answer, but Nusse looked straight at Father and said, "Do *you* know anyone down there? Have *you* seen any of the children come up here to play? Do we ever go there?"

46

"No, maybe you don't now," said Father, "but after Brit-Karen goes to live there, you will know someone to visit."

"We've never done it before," said Nusse gloomily.

"But why on earth are you moving if you're not going any farther than that?" asked Father. "I thought that you were going to another part of the country."

"Mommy wants a top," said Brit-Karen.

"What?" said Father. He didn't know what Brit-Karen meant.

"She means a top apartment," said Nusse. "They only live on the twelfth floor now."

"That's right," said Brit-Karen. "There was a top empty here and we didn't get it. We got one in the other building, so we have to move."

"Well, well, that's very sad, Brit-Karen," said Father, "but you can come and see us all the same, you know."

"Thank you very much," said Brit-Karen.

"Nusse," said Father, "you and I have a little secret, haven't we?"

"Yes," said Nusse, smiling. "It really doesn't matter so much that Brit-Karen's going to move. I'll have a lot to do with my piano lessons. I won't have much time to go out to play. It's worse for Brit-Karen." It certainly was. Brit-Karen felt lonesome when Nusse began to talk about her piano lessons.

"Cheer up," said Aurora. "Perhaps Nusse and I can meet you halfway—I mean between the buildings."

Brit-Karen looked a little brighter when she heard this.

"Where shall we go to be miserable now?" asked Nusse.

"We'll go to my place," said Brit-Karen, "because Mommy has bought some cookies for us."

They ate cookies at Brit-Karen's, and afterward Aurora

got her sled and they tobogganed on the little hill behind the block. "I'll always remember this hill," said
Brit-Karen.

Aurora didn't go home until Mother had come in from
work and the meal was ready.

"Edward," said Mother, "when do you have to defend
your thesis?"

"The seventeenth of next month," said Father.

"We'll be going to the graduates' dinner, won't we?"
said Mother.

"Yes, there usually is one," said Father.

"Will you have to dress up, Mommy?" asked Aurora.

"I'll try to make myself look as beautiful as I can,"
answered Mother, laughing.

"You ought to have your earrings, then," said Aurora.

"Yes," said Mother. "They're over there on the little
table."

"No," said Aurora, "they're not there any longer."

"Where are they, then, Aurora dear?" asked Mother.
"Are they in the bedroom?"

"No," said Aurora.

"You haven't taken them out and lost them, have you?"
asked Mother.

"Oh no," said Aurora. "Bala has eaten them."

"What?" said Mother.

"Oh dear," said Father. "It's a surprise. We have to
wait till Socrates goes to bed because he's so scared of it."

"What are we to wait for?" asked Mother.

"You'll see," said Father.

When Socrates was safely tucked into bed and fast asleep, Father brought in the vacuum cleaner. Mother certainly was surprised. She was both surprised and delighted. When she heard that Socrates had called it Bala, and that it was Bala who had swallowed her earrings, she said, "Find two old newspapers, Aurora." She unscrewed one end of the cleaner and carefully took out a bag. It was full of all the bits and pieces from the carpet.

"It was a good thing you hadn't had time to empty it down the incinerator chute," said Mother.

Now they emptied it onto an old newspaper instead. Some of the dust floated up and settled in the room again, but the earrings were there. Father rolled up the newspaper carefully and went out to the incinerator with the package of dust and crumbs.

The earrings, however, were safely in Mother's ears and didn't seem to have come to any harm from having been in Bala's tummy.

4 · A Funny Feeling

Today was Daddy's day, too. It was different from his other days. It began when he said, "Aurora, Nusse's coming for a piano lesson this morning. You remember that, don't you?"

"Yes, I do," said Aurora. "I remember it very well. Nusse has told me every time I've seen her."

"It was a strange way to get a vacuum cleaner," said Father, "but it will be fun if Nusse really wants to learn to play. She's a nice little thing, and she may have some talent."

That was the first time that day that Aurora had a funny feeling inside. Father went on talking, and the feeling went away for a little while. "You'll have to help me pay for the vacuum too," he said. "Do you know how?"

"No," said Aurora. "I've four kroner that I got for Christmas."

"You don't have to spend your money," said Father. "You'll help me by taking care of Socrates while Nusse is having her lesson. Can you do that?"

"Yes," said Aurora.

"That's fine," said Father. "You and Socrates go into the bedroom and take your cars or something else you can play with."

"Mmmm," said Aurora. She got Little Puff and three cars from her own room. She took the doll, Lille-Rora, out of Socrates's bed and sat her on the floor beside Little Puff. Father brought in the red and green and yellow bricks. Everything was ready for Socrates to play as soon as he had finished sitting on his potty.

The doorbell rang, and Socrates, Aurora, and Father went to open it.

It was Nusse. Not Nusse as she usually was, oh no; Nusse in her best dress and newly washed hair. She was so well dressed that Aurora stood and stared at her. Father looked at her, too, and said, "You're all dressed up today, Nusse."

"Yes, Mommy said to wear my best dress the first time," said Nusse. "This isn't like a plain day when I just come here to play with Aurora."

"Yes, your first piano lesson should be a special occasion," said Father. "I think it was a very good idea of your mother's."

Nusse hardly looked at Aurora. She just went and sat down at the piano. Father nodded to Aurora and Socrates and said, "Run along and play in the bedroom."

He didn't say that Aurora was to look after Socrates to help pay for the vacuum. He just told them to run along and play in the bedroom as though she was the same age as Socrates.

Aurora didn't say anything. She looked serious as she led her brother out of the room.

At first Socrates was delighted to have Aurora to play with. He hugged Little Puff and then carried him over to Aurora, saying "Little Puff Auwowa's, not Soc'ates's." He was still afraid of Little Puff, but not as much as he used to be.

"Oh thank you *so* much," said Aurora, and Socrates was highly amused. Afterward, they played with the cars for a little while. Socrates wasn't very good at that yet. He soon got tired of it. Then he heard the sound of the piano.

"Soc'ates p'ay," he said. He was remembering the day when Gran had come.

"Daddy says no," said Aurora. "He's teaching Nusse to play, you know."

Socrates thought it over. It was as if he was wondering whether he should get angry and start to cry, or whether he should show that he was pleased to have Aurora with him. At last he smiled and said, "Auwowa dear," which was what Mother often said.

"Good boy, Socrates," said Aurora, lifting him up and hugging him before she put him down again. "Now we'll build a house with your bricks."

Socrates knocked down everything she built. He became very enthusiastic about the game, and at last he was so busy in what he was doing that he had almost forgotten she was there.

Aurora wandered around the room, looked out of the window, and went over to the door. She could hear Daddy and Nusse talking. Daddy's voice sounded happy. Once he burst out laughing, and then Nusse said something, and she heard some notes played and Daddy's voice again.

It seemed so queer. Nusse sat in there and had Daddy all to herself and she, who really was Daddy's girl, had to be out here in another room. She had that funny feeling inside again. This time it was much stronger than the first time. It was something that didn't exactly hurt like a pain, but felt like a kind of heaviness inside. Everything was awful.

"Auwowa p'ay?" said Socrates, for he saw that she had gone over to the door.

"Oh, no," said Aurora. "I'm going to play with you."

"Yes," said Socrates. He went on playing with his bricks and talking to himself. Usually Aurora liked it when Socrates was busy with something and prattling away because he made so many funny sounds. But right now she wanted him to be quiet so that she could hear what Daddy and Nusse were saying.

Then she heard Daddy's voice. "That's fine, Nusse," he said. "Teaching's easy when you're so quick to learn."

Surely the half hour must be over by now. She went up to the door and put her head around it.

"Have you finished?" she asked.

"Oh no," said Father, "we've only had five minutes."

55

"Oh," said Aurora.

"Is Socrates all right?" asked Father.

"Oh, yes," said Aurora.

"Be a good girl, then, don't disturb us," said Father. "Shut the door, will you?"

"Yes," said Aurora. She went back to the bedroom and sat on the floor in front of the bricks as quiet as a mouse. Socrates looked up and saw that she was with him again, so he felt that everything was all right. Aurora sat and thought, at first for a little while and then for a long while, and then she got up quickly and went to the door. But she didn't open it. She turned around and came back to Socrates.

"Auwowa not p'ay," said Socrates. "On'y Nusse p'ay and Daddy p'ay and G'an p'ay."

Perhaps the half hour was up now. No, Daddy was still talking. There were some more notes and Nusse's voice saying, "Oh yes, I see, like that, but I can't make my little finger work right."

"You might as well practice moving it right from the start," said Father. Surely a half hour had passed now, perhaps even more. When Daddy was busy with something he often forgot what time it was. She'd better go in and tell him. What would she say? "The half hour is up?" No, that would be silly, because she wasn't absolutely sure. But she could say what Daddy often said to Mommy, "I think you're forgetting the time." She could say that. But when she stood in the doorway and saw the absorbed faces of Father and Nusse, all she said was, "Are you sure the time isn't up, Daddy?"

"Quite sure," said Father. "There're more than fifteen minutes left. Be a good girl and don't interrupt us any more."

"All right," said Aurora. She went back into the bedroom, and this time she lay under the bed, thinking. She had never known a half hour could be so long. What if there were a fire? She would have to go in and tell them. But perhaps even then Daddy would just say, "Don't disturb us, that's a good girl." Imagine Daddy having time to sit there and talk to Nusse and teach her to play the piano. Daddy, who was always so busy and had so much reading and so much housework to do.

Aurora had never thought this could happen. What if she too . . . well she didn't have a vacuum cleaner to bring him, so it wouldn't be any use.

Socrates came chasing after her under the bed. He thought it was a new game. He whispered right in her ear, but it tickled so much that Aurora crawled out the other side. Socrates followed her. They sat on the floor and looked at each other. Aurora began to talk to Socrates as if he was the same age she was. She told him quietly and seriously about everything she had been thinking of that day. "What do *you* think Socrates?" she said at last.

"Badeludoskijo boda," said Socrates. Aurora sounded so serious that he felt he had to invent a few new words as quickly as possible.

"I'll do it, then," said Aurora. "As soon as the piano lesson is over, I'll go out."

"Out," said Socrates, and smiled at her.

Then they sat for a long time and waited. At last Father opened the door and said, "Aurora and Socrates, we've finished now."

Nusse climbed down from the piano stool. "I can't stay, Aurora. I have to go upstairs and practice. Then I have to go to Brit-Karen's house and comfort her."

"Mmmm," said Aurora. That was a good thing, because Aurora didn't have time to play either.

When Nusse had gone, Father said: "Nusse seemed

to find that lesson easy. I think I'll enjoy teaching her to play. Let's see, what was I going to do next? I think it was the dishes."

"Can I go out, Daddy?" asked Aurora.

"Of course you can," he said. "I'm going to the supermarket myself today. I'll take Socrates, so you can play with your sled as long as you like."

Aurora put on her outdoor clothes.

"Have a good time, Aurora," Daddy said as she left.

"You, too," said Aurora. In her pocket was the four kroner she had been given for Christmas. Daddy hadn't noticed. He was whistling and singing. No doubt he was thinking what fun it was to teach Nusse.

Aurora went straight out of the building. She didn't stop to look up at the window to see Daddy. She usually did, and sometimes he waved to her with the table-cloth.

Aurora walked on, but Father stood at the window. "I wonder where she's going?" he said to himself. "She's in such a hurry that the sled can hardly keep up with her."

When Aurora had gone a little way, she met Brit-Karen.

"I'm moving tomorrow," said Brit-Karen.

"Oh," said Aurora.

"I'm miserable," said Brit-Karen. "Will you come home with me now?"

"No, I can't," said Aurora, "and I'm miserable myself, but Nusse's coming to see you, she told me so."

She went on, not over to the supermarket where she usually bought food, but a long way down the hill where the other stores were. They had had the piano since she was born. She had gone and looked at it every day, and sometimes she had pretended to play a note or two, but it had always seemed to be Daddy's. It was Daddy who could play it, and he did so whenever he had time.

But now that Aurora had seen Nusse sitting there playing she began to think about the piano in a different way. It was as if it were at home, calling to her.

Nusse's mother had brought Daddy a vacuum cleaner, and then Nusse had been allowed to play.

What could Aurora bring that Daddy would be very pleased with, so pleased that he would teach her to play? It should be something for the house. He had been so pleased to get the vacuum because it would help him with the housework. Aurora looked in the store window. She saw refrigerators, and different kinds of washing machines. Then she heard one woman say to another, "Oh, wouldn't it be great to have a dishwasher like that one! Just think, no more washing dishes!"

"Yes," said the other, "but I don't think washing dishes is the worst job."

"I do," said the first lady. "I think it's the very worst. I wonder what it costs—at least a few thousand kroner. . . ."

"Four kroner isn't enough," Aurora said to herself. She

stood there for a little while imagining that she was bringing the big white dishwasher home. She would need help to get it out of the store, then she could carry it on her sled. No, it would be too heavy for the sled. She would have to get the store to send it home in the delivery truck. The two men with the truck would come up in the elevator with her and help her as far as her door. Then she would say, "I can manage by myself now," and wait until they had gone. She would ring the bell. Daddy would come and open the door, and she would say, "Daddy, here is something to help you get through the housework quicker. Now maybe you'll have time to—"

"Look out, little girl!" said a voice. "We've got to fix

this window." Aurora looked up. Two workmen with ladders and tools were going to repair the top part of the big window.

Oh well. The dishwasher was too expensive, but maybe she could find something else for Daddy. She went in and walked around looking at the shelves. She looked at the beautiful red cake pans and the big white and blue breadboxes and the blue and yellow and red buckets.

There were some brushes for washing dishes hanging on the wall. Aurora remembered that Daddy said their brush at home was a sorry sight. He might like to have a new one.

"Have I enough money for a brush?" she asked a salesman.

"Yes, you have," said the man. "I'll wrap it up for you."

Aurora put it on her sled and pretended that it was terribly heavy. She had to pull with all her might. No, it was too heavy for her to pull on her own. She pretended that two people from the store would have to pull it all the way home into the elevator and along the hall, and then they could go away. When she was quite sure that the make-believe people had gone, she rang the bell. Daddy opened the door.

"A dishwasher costs too much," said Aurora, "but I've brought a brush for dishes. You can have it, and I'd really like to learn the piano, but I guess it's no use because you're so busy with Nusse—and your exam—but you can have the brush anyway."

Father looked at Aurora. It was as if he was seeing her for the first time that day. He lifted her up and carried her indoors, brush and all.

"Take your coat off," he said. "What does Socrates like doing best?"

"Emptying the sewing box," said Aurora.

"Just a minute while I take out the needles and the razor blade," said Father. "Here, Socrates, tidy this up."

Socrates could hardly believe his ears, but quietly and with great thoroughness he began to empty the sewing box. He looked so thoughtful that it was plain he was taking the job seriously.

"Now you can sit yourself at the piano, Aurora," said Father.

"Yes, but there's something else first, *you* know," said Aurora, and disappeared into her own room.

Father didn't know, but in a little while she came back wearing one of her best dresses. Not the yellow one Granny had given her at Christmas, but the red one that Father had made a little apron for, to hide the hole he had burned in it when he was ironing it. She felt that they both had a share in that one.

"Let me feel your fingers," said Father. "Goodness me, how cold they are. Come along. I'll warm them for you."

Then he and Aurora began to play.

"Can you imagine why we didn't think of this before?" said Father.

"Yes, I can," said Aurora. "You've had a lot of things to do."

"That's true," said Father, "but still we could have found time for this."

"Not before you got the dishes brush, you know," said Aurora, as she waggled her little finger up and down.

She had been practicing this all day, and anybody who noticed her would have realized that here was a little girl who was eager to learn the piano.

5 · "Little Girl in Closet"

Today was Uncle Brande's day. Mother and Father were out in the hall putting their coats and scarves on to go to work. Uncle Brande was in the bedroom playing with Socrates so that he wouldn't worry about Father going out.

Aurora stood in the hall. "Have you remembered your lunch bags?" she asked.

"Yes," said Father. "We've got them."

"Hurry or you'll be late," said Aurora. "I'll wave to you with the tablecloth."

"Have a good time, Aurora dear," said Mother.

"Remember to put on dry stockings after you've been out," said Father.

"We really must leave now, Edward," said Mother.

"Yes," said Father. "Let me see, have I got my books?"

"Have you got *yourself?*" asked Mother.

"We're off," said Father. The door shut after them. Aurora was left alone in the hall.

She stood there for a moment or two to see what it felt like, but then she remembered she had promised to wave.

It was a long time before Mother and Father got downstairs, but there they were at last. They looked up at the window, and Aurora waved the tablecloth.

They got into the car. For a minute, a lot of smoke came out of it, and then they drove off.

Aurora caught sight of something else. A big moving van stood right outside the entrance to the apartment building.

"Uncle Brande, may I go out for a little while?" she asked. "There's a moving van, and I'm sure it's Brit-Karen's."

"Of course you can go," said Uncle Brande. "Socrates and I are playing the bed-making game."

"Are you and Socrates going out, too?" said Aurora. "Later on, I mean?"

"Yes," said Uncle Brande. "What's going to happen if you come back and your feet are cold and I'm not here to let you in?"

Aurora hadn't thought of that. "Can I have the same thing as my friend Knut? Nusse uses it, too, when her mother is staying late at the shop. It looks so nice."

"You mean a door key around your neck?" said Uncle Brande. "But we've only one key, and what if I get here first?"

"Your feet might be cold too," said Aurora, and glanced down at his shoes. They weren't very new, and she didn't think they looked warm.

"Exactly," said Uncle Brande. "Can't we find a good place to hide it?"

"Under the doormat outside the door," said Aurora.

"No," said Uncle Brande. "That won't do. Everybody hides keys under mats. If someone came along who had no business here, he could let himself in and help himself from Mommy's coffee can or something."

"It's Daddy's can," said Aurora. "It was a Christmas present."

"Don't you know anyone in the building we could leave the key with?" asked Uncle Brande.

"Nusse's mother is staying late at the store today, and there's Brit-Karen, but she's moving."

"I think I've got it," said Uncle Brande. "We'll put the key under the doormat of the people next door."

"But I don't know them," said Aurora in alarm. "They just moved in."

"That doesn't matter," said Uncle Brande. "We won't tell them."

"Yes, but what if a burglar comes and finds the key there?" said Aurora.

"It won't fit that door," said Uncle Brande, "and he'll never guess that it belongs to this apartment."

"That's a good idea," said Aurora. "Will you help me with my boots, Uncle Brande?"

"Of course," said Uncle Brande, but he was so strong, he pulled the laces until it felt as if her feet couldn't breathe.

He had to do it again. "You're all right now, young lady," he said. "Let's get Socrates ready while we're about it."

"Daddy?" said Socrates and darted into the kitchen. "Daddy gone," he said to himself. Then he rushed out of the kitchen and into Aurora's room. "Daddy," he said again. He went into the bathroom and then into the bedroom. That was where he had been when Daddy left. They had thought they were smart not to let Socrates see Daddy going out. They were wrong. Because they hadn't

68

told him, Socrates was running around looking for Daddy now. When Uncle Brande tried to put Socrates's boots on, he kept shrieking "Daddy." At last he was sure that Daddy couldn't hear him, and he would only go to Aurora. Gran had been there one day, and Daddy had been there two days. Nobody had explained that Uncle Brande would be here today *instead* of Daddy. Socrates had thought that Uncle Brande had come to play with Daddy. Daddy had gone, but Aurora was here. She had been here every day, and now he clung to her.

"Can you dress him?" said Uncle Brande. He looked thoroughly unhappy.

"Yes, of course, cheer up," said Aurora. "I'll talk to him."

"Maybe I can finish the dishes," said Uncle Brande.

"We've got a new brush," said Aurora, smiling. "Just think, Socrates, Uncle Brande has come all this way to look after us."

"Uncle Bwande wash dishes," said Socrates.

"Yes, and then he'll go for a walk," said Aurora.

"Soc'ates, too, Soc'ates go walk."

When Socrates was ready, Uncle Brande whispered, "Do you think we could borrow your red sled?"

"Yes," said Aurora. "I'm only going to watch the moving van today."

They put the key in its hiding place and went out. Socrates and Uncle Brande had to stop and look at the

moving van for a little while because it was so big, but
Socrates started to pull the sled away, so Uncle Brande
gave Aurora a nod and hurried after him. The big moving van was almost full. After the last chair had been
put in, Brit-Karen and her mother appeared. They were
each carrying a potted plant. Nusse came behind them,
and she had *two* potted plants. She followed the others
to a car in front of the moving van.

Brit-Karen looked up at Building Z and said, "I don't
want to move."

Her father, who was already sitting at the wheel of
the car, shouted, "Hurry up, Brit-Karen. We want to get
there before the furniture!"

"Sit here beside me," said her mother, pulling her into
the back seat. They were still holding the potted plants.

The door slammed, the car drove away, and Brit-Karen had gone. Nusse looked around and saw Aurora.

"It's a good thing you're here," she said, "because I can be your best friend now."

"Oh," said Aurora, taken aback. She couldn't find anything else to say.

"What do you want to do now?" said Nusse.

Aurora thought it wouldn't be easy, being best friends with Nusse. She might always be the one to have to think of things to do. Suddenly Aurora felt terribly sorry that Brit-Karen had moved. She said, "Let's pretend Brit-Karen has been kidnapped. We'll go down to her new apartment and rescue her."

"How did you think of that?" said Nusse. "It's a great idea. Brit-Karen didn't want to move one bit. Did you see how pale she was? Her daddy knew it, and that's why he drove off so quickly. We must rescue her."

"We'll do it secretly," said Aurora, "and move very quietly."

"Creep along," said Nusse. "That will make it more exciting."

"Yes," whispered Aurora.

"I'm sure that Brit-Karen can stay with us," said Nusse, "but then she'll have to be my best friend again."

"That's okay," said Aurora. "She can stay with us, too." But as soon as she had said it, she wasn't sure. It was so awkward when Daddy was away so much.

"She can live in our kitchen cupboard," said Nusse. "That's a good hiding place."

"Yes, and I can bring her food sometimes," said Aurora.

"Yes, food costs a lot," said Nusse. "You spend everything you earn on food, and a little more as well. Mommy found that out," she added suddenly, "from working in the supermarket. Brit-Karen had better stay with you. Your closet would be a good place."

"All right," said Aurora. She was so excited she felt a weight inside her, but it wasn't the same kind of feeling she had had when Nusse was sitting with Daddy and playing the piano.

They were quite a long way from their own building by now. Neither of them spoke again. They just crept along, looking mysterious.

"It's a good thing there's only one way up here," said Nusse, looking at the tall apartment building that was just as high as Building Z.

"Yes," said Aurora. Her voice sounded uncertain. It was strange to be outside a building she didn't know at all. A few children were standing around. Nusse pretended to be in a big hurry and went quickly through the door with Aurora in tow.

"They've got an elevator," said Aurora.

"Yes, and Brit-Karen said they were having a top apartment," said Nusse, "so we can just take the elevator all the way up."

"Yes," said Aurora. It wasn't long before the elevator had carried them up to the top floor. They came out into a long hall with lots and lots of doors. Which door was Brit-Karen's?

It was easy to find it, because it was the only door with no nameplate on it. They couldn't go in with no excuse, because if they did they might not even get a chance to talk to Brit-Karen on this busy moving day.

"Ask if we can borrow some sugar," said Nusse. "You do it, Aurora. They know my mommy's not home."

"Mmmm," said Aurora. "I'll ask for some salt instead. Then they won't think it's just for us to eat."

"That's a good idea," said Nusse, and rang the bell.

Brit-Karen's mother opened the door. "Well I never," she said. "Are you here already?"

"No," said Aurora, "I . . . I . . ."

"She just wants to ask if she can borrow two teaspoonfuls of salt," said Nusse.

"The van isn't here yet," said Brit-Karen's mother. "I think the moving men stopped for lunch. Come in for a moment since you're here, but I can't have you here for long today."

"No, of course not," said Nusse. Brit-Karen appeared. Her face lit up when she saw them.

"This apartment is almost like the one you had before," said Nusse.

"There's an extra cupboard in the kitchen, and there's a green bathroom," said Brit-Karen.

"Show them your room," said her mother.

Nusse whispered, "Aurora and I are rescuing you. You're going to stay with Aurora and hide in her closet. We'll both bring you food, because we know you didn't want to move."

"No, I didn't," said Brit-Karen.

"Hurry up," said Nusse, "and let's go."

"Mommy, I'm going with Aurora and Nusse," said Brit-Karen.

"All right, there's nothing to do here anyway," said her mother, "but later on I'll want you to help me."

As soon as the three of them were outside the building, they ran as fast as they could.

Uncle Brande and Socrates weren't home yet.

"Shut your eyes," Aurora said, "and don't look until I tell you."

Nusse and Brit-Karen were surprised, but they did as they were told. Aurora got the key from under the mat next door. "We can unlock the door now," she said.

They went straight into Aurora's room.

"There you are, you see," said Nusse. "You'll have plenty of room in Aurora's closet."

"Yes," said Brit-Karen. She didn't look happy.

"Wait there a moment," said Nusse. "I have to go home for something." While she was gone, Uncle Brande and Socrates came in.

"Hello, Aurora," said Uncle Brande, "Are you back already? Were you cold?"

"Oh no," said Aurora. She pushed Brit-Karen further into the closet.

"Don't shut the door," whispered Brit-Karen. A moment later, the bell rang. Uncle Brande went and opened the front door. "Hello, Miss Nusse," he said. "Do you want to see Aurora?"

"Yes," said Nusse. She had half a loaf of bread under her arm and a bottle of cod-liver oil in her hand. She tried to hide them behind her back, but Uncle Brande

had seen them already. "Are you going hiking?" he asked.

"Oh no, I'm just going to have my lunch here," said Nusse. "I brought some food with me because I know you haven't got very much money."

"Quite right," said Uncle Brande, smiling in his shaggy beard. "That was a kind thought. The best part is I'd forgotten to buy bread today, so it's a good thing you brought some. We'll only borrow it, of course. Aurora can go and buy two loaves after we eat."

"Little girl in closet," said Socrates.

"Oh yes," said Uncle Brande. "You're going to have some lunch now, Socrates."

He cut the bread and buttered it. Aurora and Nusse carefully put every other slice in their laps. Then they excused themselves and went in to see Brit-Karen.

Brit-Karen wasn't uncomfortable in the closet, but it was boring. She began to wonder whether the moving van had arrived yet. It might be fun to be there and put her room in order. She was going to have a new carpet, too. . . .

Nusse disappeared again from the table. "Why on earth are the two of you running back and forth all the time?" asked Uncle Brande. Aurora didn't know what to say. Now it sounded as if Nusse had two voices. "I don't want cod-liver oil," said one voice. "No one would," said the other voice, "but while you're here you'll have to have it. We can't afford to give you hamburgers all day long. If you have some cod-liver oil, you'll be on the safe side, that's what Mommy says."

"Does Nusse want to be an actress?" asked Uncle Brande. "Is she practicing using two voices at once?"

The doorbell rang. It was Nusse's mother. "I thought you'd be here," she said. "Can you come and help me now?"

"Nusse was kind enough to lend us half a loaf of bread," said Uncle Brande. "I'll pay you back as soon as Aurora goes to the supermarket."

"That's all right," said Nusse's mother. "Too bad I didn't know. I've just come from the supermarket. I work there, and I could have brought you some bread."

"Aurora will do it," said Uncle Brande. "Nusse, don't forget your bottle of cod-liver oil."

"Cod-liver oil?" said Nusse's mother. "Are you carrying that around with you?"

"Yes, I thought I'd have a little. I was so thirsty," said Nusse.

"Well, I don't know what's come over the child. Come along now," said her mother. Nusse went off, looking back at Aurora.

"That's that," said Uncle Brande. "Aurora, be a good girl and go to the supermarket for me, will you? I'd like some flour, too."

He helped Aurora on with her coat. There was no chance to tell Brit-Karen. However, Aurora managed to turn the key of her room as she went by and take it with her. At least there was no chance of anyone discovering Brit-Karen. Aurora had never run so fast to the supermarket. Even so, a great deal happened while she was away.

Uncle Brande was scrubbing potatoes when all of a sudden he thought he heard strange noises coming from Aurora's room.

"Little girl in closet," said Socrates, certainly for the tenth time.

At last Uncle Brande seemed to understand. He tried to get into Aurora's room, but the door was locked. The doorbell rang again. Brit-Karen's mother stood there. "Is Brit-Karen here?" she asked.

Uncle Brande looked at the locked bedroom door. How was he going to say that a little girl might be in there but he wasn't sure who it was, and unfortunately the door was locked?

"Aurora's at the supermarket," he said. "Come in and sit down." Uncle Brande had no idea what to talk about, but luckily Brit-Karen's mother was quite sociable. The time went quickly until the bell rang again. Uncle Brande shot up like a rocket. "Open your door, Aurora. Her mother's here. I didn't say anything but. . . ."

Aurora got the key and unlocked the door. Brit-Karen stood there with her hat and coat on.

"Come along," said Uncle Brande, and led the two small girls into the living room.

"Oh, there you are," said Brit-Karen's mother. "It's time to come home with me. Aurora will visit us when we have unpacked. I've been to our old apartment and had a talk with the woman who is cleaning it. Good-bye, and thank you very much for having Brit-Karen."

"It was nothing," said Uncle Brande. Brit-Karen looked as if she agreed with him, but she didn't say anything.

When Father came home, he said, "Did anything happen today?"

"Well . . ." said Uncle Brande.

"Oh yes, lots of things," said Aurora, "but I must ask Nusse first if I can tell you."

"Little girl in closet," said Socrates. "Daddy not go."

"You'll have to tell Socrates when you're going out," said Uncle Brande, "so he won't be upset."

"Little girl in closet," said Socrates again. Aurora thought she would have to tell Daddy everything that evening, for he looked so bewildered. But one thing was certain: she would never rescue Brit-Karen again. Brit-Karen herself wouldn't mind. Not for anything in the world did she want to live in Aurora's closet. She would rather live in the new apartment.

Socrates didn't forget the day so easily. He went into Aurora's room. "Little girl in closet," he said, expectantly. He was a little disappointed and a little relieved when he found no one there.

"Little girl in closet gone," he said.

6 · Something to Hang on the Wall

Father sat in a chair and stared gloomily in front of him. Aurora nearly asked him what was the matter several times, but she didn't dare. He looked terrible. At last she said, "Are you worried about the exam?"

"Er—no, I mean yes, of course I am, but I'm taking it of my own free will. This is something else," said Father.

"What is it?" asked Aurora. "Is it something awful?"

"Yes it is," said Father. "I need a picture of myself. Bring me the old album, Aurora. Maybe there's a picture there I've forgotten."

Aurora was pleased. She loved to sit and look at the old photos of Daddy when he was a little boy and lived with Granny.

"Put it here on the table," said Father. "Where shall we begin?"

"We'll begin at the very beginning," said Aurora.

"All right," said Father, "but I can't very well use pictures taken when I was a baby."

"We'll begin at the beginning all the same," said Aurora.

There was a picture of a little baby lying on a sheepskin rug, and another of a young lady holding a baby in her arms. The young lady was Granny, and under the picture was "OUR SON." Aurora looked at the two pictures for a long time before she turned the page. There was Daddy, aged two, with a mass of curls. "Oh, you do look sweet," she said. "You're like Socrates. Is it Socrates?"

"No, it's me," said Father. "I don't remember anything about it, but I know it's me."

"Yes," said Aurora, "Granny said so."

"I remember that one, though," said Father, "because I was bigger and my father had made me a horse."

"You don't have so many curls in that one," said Aurora.

"No, I'd had my hair cut," said Father.

They looked at several pictures, and at last Father had got so big that he had started to go to school and had lost two front teeth, but he was smiling just the same. He got bigger and bigger, and finally he was a full-grown schoolboy and then an undergraduate.

"I can use that one," said Father. "We'll take that one out, Aurora, and ask Mommy what she thinks."

But when Mother saw it she said, "No, Edward, you

can't use a photograph that was taken so many years ago. You hardly look grown-up. Now you're going to go and have one taken. If it comes out well, it will be a reminder of the time when you got your degree."

"Yes, but suppose I don't get it?" said Father.

"We'll have the picture anyway," said Mother. "And I've just had a good idea. We'll come with you and have a picture taken of all four of us, because we don't have one."

"Do you mean one of those family groups?" said Father.

"Yes," said Mother, "that's exactly what I do mean."

"You proudly hang it on the wall, and a hundred years later people who see it say, 'How funny they look!' " said Father.

"Edward," said Mother, "are we all lucky to have each

other or are we not? I want to have a picture of us all *now*, and when you and I are old we'll look at it and say, 'Oh, how happy we were then!' "

"Aren't we going to be happy when we're old?" asked Father.

"Of course we are," said Mother, "But it's nice to look at such pictures. We'll feel as if we're living that day all over again."

Father didn't have the slightest desire to live that day over again. He hated having his picture taken.

But Mother was so enthusiastic there was no getting out of it. He brushed his hair and shined his shoes, and Mother put on a pretty dress. Socrates and Aurora put on their best clothes, and off they went to the photographer's.

"Why not take the car?" said Father. "I feel silly walking along in my best clothes."

"A little fresh air will do you good," said Mother. "You're very pale. You stay indoors reading too much. Your brain needs oxygen."

Socrates was the only one who was allowed to ride. He would rather have walked, but there wasn't time, because they had to get to the photographer's before he closed.

"We may be too late," said Father.

"I made an appointment," said Mother. "It will be all right, you'll see."

"I suppose so," said Father.

"You'd better have one taken on your own first," said Mother.

When they arrived at the photographer's, they went into a little waiting room. There were pegs on the wall to hang coats on and a long mirror they could see themselves in. A lady came and told them they would have to wait a little while because the photographer was busy with a customer, but he would soon be ready.

They heard the photographer's voice, "Smile, please."

"I don't want to," said a voice which they were sure they recognized.

"Do you want to look disagreeable?" asked the photographer.

"I don't like smiling when I've nothing to smile about," said the voice.

"All right, just as you please," said the photographer. "Shall we take you in profile, or full face?"

"I think we'll try both ways," was the answer.

"All right," said the photographer. "Perhaps you would take off your head scarf?"

"No, it wouldn't look like me."

"Yes, but if you want a kind of passport photograph I think you'll have to take off your scarf. The police insist that the person in the photograph should be seen as clearly as possible."

"I haven't told you what it's for," said the voice, "but

I'll do it for two pictures and put my scarf on for the others."

"Look up," said the photographer.

"I can't look straight into the lamp."

"No, just up a little and to the side," said the photographer. "Think of something pleasant."

"Yes," came the answer. The camera clicked away, and at last the photographer said, "That was fine. What were you thinking about?"

"I'll tell you next week," said the voice. "Is that all?"

"Yes. You'll have the pictures in five days' time."

"Could I have them before that?"

"Oh yes," said the photographer. "If you're in a hurry, you can pick them up on Friday."

"That's very nice of you," said the voice.

A few minutes went by. The curtain was pulled aside. Out came Gran.

Now, of course, Mother and Father and Aurora and Socrates knew that Gran was there, because they recognized her voice. They were prepared. But Gran had no idea that they had been sitting there, so she was rather taken aback.

"So you've had your picture taken, Gran," said Mother. "How nice! Each of your grandchildren will be able to have one. I hope you'll let us order one, too."

"We'd better see what that fellow has made of it first," said Gran.

85

The photographer looked almost scared. Gran had certainly got out of bed the wrong side today.

"I believe you're as cross as Daddy when he has his picture taken," said Mother.

"I didn't have it taken for fun," said Gran. "Things will soon be warming up," she added to Father.

"I thought as much," he said.

"Sh!" said Gran. "Don't say anything, because it might not turn out all right. . . ."

"It's the same with me," said Father. "The worst of it is that lots of people know what I'm going to do, but practically no one knows that you. . . ."

"Just you and Aurora and one other," said Gran.

"Who's that?" asked Father.

"Our Morten," said Gran. "He and I have had secrets together before, and I don't want to keep him in the dark now."

"We must cross our fingers for each other," said Father. "I'm sure it will be all right, you'll see."

"We'll have to take things as they come," said Gran. She nodded to the others and went out.

"Well, it's your turn now," said the photographer.

Father was to have his picture taken first. The other three stayed in the waiting room. Aurora glanced at Mother. She looked worried.

They could hear the photographer talking to Father. "Try not to look so angry," he said. "There's no point in waving teddy bears and toy ducks at *you*. You have to show a little cooperation."

Aurora peeped through a little gap in the curtain. Daddy was sitting looking like a thundercloud.

"You don't need to smile, exactly," said the photographer, "but please don't look so cross."

Father wasn't cross. He was frowning because he was embarrassed. Nothing on earth would have made him feel at ease just then.

The photographer paced up and down.

"Just a minute," he said. "I'm just going to get some more film." He had to go through the room where Aurora, Socrates, and Mother were waiting. Mother beckoned to him and whispered something in his ear.

He nodded and went back with a new roll of film which he put in his camera.

"You can relax," he said. "Your wife says that you can use your student photograph after all."

Father smiled a smile of genuine relief. The photographer clicked away and said, "Yes, that's all right, but you have to be in the family group."

"Very well," said Father. His face fell again, and the photographer said quickly, "Would you hold the little boy in your lap?" He thought that Father would be too busy to remember that his picture was being taken.

Somebody else who couldn't be depended on to cooperate was Socrates. He had been happy enough when they decided to go out so suddenly. He thought it was silly to put his best clothes on, but he didn't object. He got a little annoyed, though, when he wasn't allowed to walk but had to ride in the stroller. Mother and Father had said they were in a hurry just as though he couldn't walk very fast if he wanted to.

Now the photographer began to wave toy ducks and teddy bears at him and call out "he, he, ha, ha," every other minute. Socrates grew quieter and quieter. Aurora could see that he was getting angry. Then he became frightened and began to cry. At first he cried quietly, and then louder and louder, while the tears rolled down his cheeks. Father wiped them away with a big white handkerchief.

Mother was in despair. Here was the family group that she and Father were to look at when they were old, and all of them were either cross or unhappy.

It wouldn't do. The photographer was trying hard and meant well with his carrying on. Aurora thought he had to be told, so she went up to him and caught hold of his coat and said, "Sh! You mustn't talk so loudly. It frightens Socrates. Just whisper, and then hide behind that black cloth. Socrates likes playing peekaboo." The photographer looked at Socrates's woebegone face. Then he looked at Aurora. "I'm glad you told me," he sighed.

Aurora went back to her place, and the photographer began to whisper. Socrates listened as hard as he could.

When that man wasn't yelling he wasn't afraid any longer, and when the man dived behind the black cloth and Socrates could still see his legs, he began to smile. The man was playing peekaboo, but he wasn't any good at hiding.

"There," said Socrates, pointing. "Click" went the camera. The photographer came out from under the black cloth and began to whisper again. By now Mother and Father were so amused that they hardly could sit still. In the next picture they laughed out loud, and Aurora sternly shhhed them.

Then it was all over and they could go home.

A few days later, Mother went and picked up the photographs. Father was surprised and pleased when he saw the picture of himself.

"It's the best picture you've ever had taken," said Mother. "You can use that in the newspapers."

"However did he get me to look so happy?" said Father.

"That's a secret," said Mother.

The picture that Mother was going to look at when she was old was a very fine one, too. She bought a frame for it and hung it on the wall, and every day Socrates stood in front of it and said, "There's Soc'ates." So he enjoyed the picture without waiting until he was old at all.

7 · "We're Not Cows!"

Father's picture appeared in the newspaper. Mother and Father and Aurora and Socrates sat up in bed and looked at it.

"Now the fun will begin," said Father. "You won't see very much of me for a while. I'm moving to a room in town."

"Won't you come back at night, either?" asked Aurora in alarm.

"No, Daddy needs peace and quiet to work," said Mother.

So many exciting things were going on that she could hardly stand it, thought Aurora. Everything was happening at once. First, Daddy left home and went away with two suitcases. Of course it wasn't for always, only for two weeks. During that time he had to write something called a paper. The people at the university told him that he had two weeks to write this paper. When the time was up he was to come and read them what he had written. He had to do other things, too, but this was the first thing, and so it was no wonder that he needed peace and quiet. He had borrowed Uncle Brande's one-room apartment. Uncle Brande went off to the little hut where he usually spent the summer. He said it was very nice in spring, too.

Who would take care of Aurora and Socrates now that both Uncle Brande and Daddy were away? Gran?

No, Gran had almost as much to do as Daddy. When she wasn't going into town to have a driving lesson, she sat in her bedroom for most of the day reading the highway code. No, somebody else was going to look after Aurora and Socrates. That was Granny, Aurora and Socrates's own grandmother, and Granny's friend Putten was coming with her.

Today, Aurora and Socrates were to go to the station with Mommy to meet them. Then Mommy was going on to the office while everyone else went home to Tiriltoppen.

"Suppose they don't come?" said Aurora when they got to the station. "Socrates and I will have to go home by ourselves."

"They'll come," said Mother.

"You've been here before, Socrates," said Aurora. "Once when you were a baby, and once when we went to Granny's for Christmas."

"Wide in twain," said Socrates.

"Now we must wait until the train comes," said Mother. "Look at that funny little train, Socrates."

Socrates had a good look at everything. He pulled at Mother's skirt and said again, "Wide in twain."

"Yes, soon," said Mother. She began to get nervous. Socrates was in an energetic mood, and it wasn't likely he'd be willing to wait much longer. A voice came from the loudspeaker saying the train would be ten minutes late.

"Oh dear," said Mother. "I won't have much time to talk to them before I have to go."

If only the train would come! thought Aurora. It was always a little upsetting when Mommy was short of time.

Socrates was ready to lose his temper. He couldn't see any train, and he noticed that Mother was nervous. Should he sit down and yell or should he try running away from them? The second idea would be most fun. He broke away from Mother and darted off as fast as his little legs could carry him.

"Run after him, Aurora," said Mother.

Mother was carrying a heavy briefcase, so it wasn't so easy for her to run quickly, but she also went after him as fast as she could.

Usually Aurora had no difficulty in catching Socrates, but here there were lots of people with suitcases and backpacks in the way, and Socrates ran in and out of them all. At last she caught him, but Socrates wasn't having any. He lay down and kicked and screamed until he deafened the people around him and drowned the voice of the loudspeaker.

"Shall we play train?" said Aurora. "You can be the engine."

Socrates thought about it. Then he nodded and said, "Mommy too. Soc'ates engine, and Mommy twain and Auwowa twain."

"All right," said Aurora. "I'll be a passenger car, and Mommy can be a baggage car because she has a lot to carry."

They came back to Mother and Aurora whispered, "You have to be a baggage car or he'll get angry again."

Mother looked around. There were a lot of people here and she had a heavy briefcase, but it would be impossible if Socrates had a tantrum now. He looked at her expectantly. She took her place behind Aurora, and he beamed and said "Toot toot!" and went puffing away through the crowd. It wasn't exactly a slow train. Mother and Aurora had to run to keep up with the lively engine.

The people who were waiting for their trains to arrive had something to look at. Even though the baggage car wasn't very happy when she moved off, at least it was better than having the engine lying on the ground screaming.

Oddly enough, the time passed very quickly when Mother was a baggage car, and the loudspeaker announced that the train was coming in.

"We have to stop being trains now, Socrates," said Mother. "Here comes the train with Granny and Putten."

Socrates held her hand and stood quite still, for the real train was big and seemed to be coming straight at them. Aurora was anxious. Suppose they weren't on the train? Suppose Granny had overslept? One carriage window after another went by, and she couldn't see them. Suddenly Mother started to wave. There in the doorway stood Putten, waving harder still, for she was afraid they wouldn't see her.

Granny was there, too. "Isn't Edward here?" she asked.

"He's left home," said Aurora.

"It's obvious the boy must get on with his work, but who is going to carry our suitcase?" said Granny. "Putten and I decided to have one case between us, but it's so heavy we can hardly lift it."

"We'll find somebody to help us," said Mother. She beckoned to a man with a cart. But as soon as Granny and Putten had got out of the train, Socrates darted into it.

"No, Socrates," said Mother. "You're going home now."

"Soc'ates wide in twain," he said.

"Oh dear, and I have to leave," said Mother. "What shall we do?"

"We'll manage all right," said Granny. "You go, Marie. Aurora and I and the porter will go to the taxi stand, and Putten can play trains with Socrates for a minute or two. You know where the taxis are, don't you, Putten?"

"Oh, yes," said Putten. She got into the train again, and Socrates got in with her. He remembered Putten from their Christmas visit and he liked to play with her. A minute or two later the others could see Socrates and Putten looking out of the window and waving to them.

Mother went off to work, and Granny and Aurora joined the line for a taxi. But time passed, and there was no sign of Socrates and Putten.

"What on earth are they doing?" said Granny. "It's

time Putten stopped playing trains. You'd better go and look for them, Aurora."

"All right," said Aurora. She didn't feel very brave about going into the big station by herself, but it was no good thinking about it. She had to find her brother. Granny couldn't leave her suitcase, because someone might take it if they could manage to carry it.

There was a lot of noise and bustle in the station, many people talking to each other, luggage going by on carts, and the loudspeaker giving out announcements. The announcements were the worst part. They seemed much louder now that Aurora was alone. They were so loud that she could hardly think. To get to the trains you had to go through some small gates. A ticket collector was sitting in a little house beside them. But several trains had come in and she couldn't remember where Granny's train had been. She stood still for a moment or two. If only Putten and Socrates would come now, she wouldn't need to know which train it was. If only Daddy had finished his exam and was home again! If he were here now, everything would be fine. He would tell her about the places the trains were going to, and it would all be exciting.

But Daddy wasn't here. The trains seemed to be standing there staring at her. Which one should she choose? Perhaps she could say "Eeny meeny miney mo." "Eeny, meeny, miney, mo, catch a robber by his toe, if he hollers let him go, O, U, T spells OUT." Yes, that train looked like a nice one.

"You have a ticket, young lady?" said a ticket collector, who was sitting inside his little house.

"I only want to look for my brother and a lady," said Aurora.

"All right, run along then," said the man.

Aurora walked along beside the train. A lot of people were sitting in it, so maybe it wasn't only Socrates who wanted to play trains. But Aurora soon realized that this was different, for the train was so full that it must be ready to go. Supposing it went back to Bessby with Putten and Socrates in it?

Now Aurora knew what to do. She would ask the ticket collector where the train from Bessby was. But when she came back, he wasn't there any more because the train was leaving. She went up to another railwayman. "Can you tell me where the train from Bessby is?" she asked.

"From Bessby?" said the man. "There's no train that starts from there, but there is a station called Bessby. The train that came through it is over there, but it won't be leaving again for hours. It just came in. Surely you're not traveling by yourself and waiting all that time?"

"I'm looking for someone," said Aurora.

"There won't be anyone there now," said the man. "It came in fifteen minutes ago."

"They *are* there, I hope," said Aurora and ran through the gate.

She passed one carriage after another—all empty. Every time she came to another window she thought, "They'll be here," but they weren't. The train was very long. She had come to a freight car now, the sort of train car that had big doors in the middle and no windows.

She was just about to turn back when all at once she thought she heard knocking and shouting.

"Hello, hello, we're not cows!"

It was Putten's voice.

"Hello," said Aurora. "Can you hear me, Putten?"

"Yes," said Putten. "Socrates and I are in here, and

some idiot has shut the door and I can't get it open."

"I'll tell the man," shouted Aurora, and ran back.

"Please, you must help us," she said.

"Are you here again?" said the man. "I guess you didn't find the people you were looking for."

"Yes, I did," said Aurora. "I heard them. They're inside a train car, and they're shouting that they're not cows. You have to come and help me to open the door."

"What are you talking about?" said the man. "You must be good at making up stories."

"Oh no," said Aurora, "but they're in there now, Putten and Socrates."

"I've never heard of such a thing," said the man, shaking his head. "Imagine sending a child here on her own."

"I'm not on my own," said Aurora. "Granny's in line for a taxi, and Putten and Socrates are playing trains, but now they've become cows instead and can't get out."

She kept tugging at him, and at last he strolled over to the train with her. He looked in all the passenger cars, just as she had done. "They're not here," she said, "they're much further on."

At last they came to the baggage cars. Suddenly the man's expression changed. "Sh!" he said, although Aurora hadn't said a word.

"Will somebody come at once and open this door for us! We're not cows. There aren't any cows here, just two people, a big one and a small one."

"Well, my word!" said the man. He unlocked the door

17954

and pushed it to one side. There stood Putten and Socrates.

"How in the world did you get here?" asked the man. "Have you been traveling without a ticket?"

"No, indeed," said Putten, "but Socrates wanted to have a ride in the train, so we did that first. Then we wanted something else to do that was more fun, so I told him how cows often go on the train and ride in cattle cars. Socrates wanted us to pretend we were cows, so we went into a freight car and stood in a corner, and pretended we were eating. Somebody came and slammed the door. They were making so much noise and talking so loudly they didn't hear us shout."

"Well, you can thank this little girl that you didn't have to stay in your cattle car until late at night," said the man. "Imagine a grown-up acting like that!"

"Yes, imagine," said Putten, and got out. The man lifted Socrates down.

"Moo," said Socrates, and wanted to get in again, but Aurora said, "We're going home now to have something to eat."

Socrates thought about it. He was hungry. It was a good idea to go home and have some food, even if he was a cow.

Granny worried as she sat on her big suitcase and waited for the others. Her turn for a taxi had come a long time ago, but that couldn't be helped. She wondered if she should carry the heavy case back into the station and look for them herself, or if she should go to the stationmaster's office and ask him to call Aurora and Socrates and Putten over the loudspeaker.

Luckily she waited a little longer, and the three of them appeared.

"Where *have* you been?" said Granny.

"We've had a ride in the train," said Putten. She didn't say anything else because she didn't want to explain that she had been pretending to be a cow. Socrates kept saying "moo, moo," but Granny didn't realize why. Whether they were cows or people, they were all glad to get home to Tiriltoppen. Aurora was sure that she would never go to the station again unless Mommy or Daddy was there to look after Socrates and Putten.

8 · Whispering through the Mailbox

Things weren't what they used to be, thought Socrates. Granny and Putten were sleeping in the bedroom instead of Mommy and Daddy. In Aurora's room they had put a funny kind of bed with a drawer underneath it. Mommy was sleeping there, not in the drawer, of course, but in the bed.

During the day when Mother was out, Putten and Granny took care of Socrates and gave him his meals. He knew them and that was a good thing, but now and again he remembered that it was Daddy who really should have been there. Then he got on his hands and knees and peered under the chairs to see if Daddy had hidden there.

At least Aurora was at home, when she wasn't out playing with Nusse. Mother was away a lot. First of all she went to the office, and then when she had been at home for a little while she acted very strange. She hurried about the kitchen with a basket on her arms, putting eggs and butter and bread and coffee into it. When Mother was ready to go out, Granny always came into the hall and said, "Tell him not to sit there and freeze. He's got his woolen jacket with him, I suppose?"

"Oh, yes," said Mother, "but I'll tell him all the same." Then she went away. It was a lucky thing that Aurora was at home. Otherwise Putten and Granny wouldn't have known what Socrates was used to at bedtime. It was simple enough to say that he just had a bath, ate his dinner, and went to bed. But the first evening that Granny and Putten took care of him, he screamed until he must have been heard on all the thirteen floors of their building.

Aurora had to explain the way in which Socrates had his bath, ate his dinner, and went to bed.

First of all, Father would say, "I'm going to turn on the bath water now, Socrates." This was a kind of signal for Socrates. He crawled under the bench at full speed.

He lay there as quiet as a mouse and waited. Now and then he gave a little giggle, at the thought of what was going to happen. When the bath was ready, Father got down on his hands and knees and sang "The Teddy Bears' Picnic": *di da di da di di da di da di da di di da di da*. While he sang, he crawled around looking for Socrates. He knew that Socrates was under the bench, but he looked into the bedroom and into the kitchen. When he came near the bench he sang a little louder, and it was so exciting that Socrates shrieked with delight. Then Father said in surprise: "Oh, is *that* where you are?"

Father did a few extra turns around the living room, and Socrates came out of his hiding place by himself and climbed onto Father's back and rode into the bathroom.

There he had to be undressed. That sounded easy, too, but it had to be done in a special way.

First his jersey came off, and then Socrates put his finger on Father's nose, and then his trousers came off, and Socrates did a few exercises on Father's lap and stretched his legs up and tickled the tip of his own nose with his foot.

Then came the bath. Father washed Socrates's hair. Socrates lay with his head back, and Daddy had to sing a very special song that he had made up once when Socrates panicked because he had water in his ears. The song went like this: " 'Baa baa baa,' said the baby lamb, 'maa maa maa,' said his father the ram; 'moo,' said the calf, 'I'm a fine little fellow,' and his father, the bull, gave a great big bellow."

Socrates wanted to hear about all these animals, and Father had to be careful not to wash his hair so quickly that he had finished before the song ended.

Then the rest of him had to be washed, and now and

again Father pulled him through the water like a little fish. After that, Socrates was allowed to play with a boat for a little while, and finally Father lifted him out and wrapped him in a big bath towel and dried one toe at a time, telling a little story about each of them.

Poor Granny and Putten knew nothing about all this. Aurora had to be there the whole time and show them what to do. It was Putten who had to crawl around on all fours and look for Socrates, because Granny was too stiff. But Putten couldn't sing, and certainly not "The Teddy Bears' Picnic." Luckily Granny could, so she sang while Putten crawled.

When they got to the hair-washing part, they tried singing "My Goat Bluey," but Socrates wouldn't have it— at least he was willing to have it later on, but not while his hair was being washed. So Aurora had to teach them the other song, but by then the bath water was nearly cold. However, Socrates was not unreasonable. He realized that it took time for Putten and Granny to get used to their new duties. As the days went by, he allowed them to have some ideas of their own and didn't get angry if their way of doing things was different from Father's.

They were so busy that there wasn't much time to think about what Aurora was used to. That didn't matter so much, because Aurora put herself to bed, and then she pretended that Father was home and was sitting beside her bed and talking to her about the ancient Greeks or perhaps telling her a fairy story.

One evening Granny heard Aurora talking in her room, and when she looked in, she found that Aurora was pretending to talk to her Father. So Granny came in and began to tell her about Father when he was a little boy. After she had done this for several evenings she told Aurora about the time when she herself was a little girl. Aurora almost liked this better.

Mother didn't come home late the first evening. She had only gone into town to see that there was something for Father to eat in Uncle Brande's apartment. She thought she would have a chat with Granny and Putten before she went to bed. They had managed to deal with Socrates and to talk to Aurora, but they were so worn out that they had to go to bed immediately afterward. Mother hadn't realized that they would be so tired. The next day they were full of energy again, and quite eager for Mother to go because they were so proud of being able to take care of Aurora and Socrates on their own.

One morning, Mother had gone to the office and Granny was busy with Socrates and the housework. Aurora was in her own room explaining to her doll Little Puff why Father was away. She had done this many times before, but Little Puff couldn't understand why Father couldn't be at home at night even though he had to study during the day.

"He's only got two weeks, you see," said Aurora, "so he has to work at night, too."

She made her bed, and when she had finished, she put Little Puff on the quilt so he could look around the room. She started to go into the kitchen to help Putten with the dishes, but when she came into the hall she heard a funny noise. There was a scraping and whispering, and she clearly heard someone say very softly, "Aurora." At first she was scared. It was very strange. When she had looked around and listened carefully, she discovered that the sound came from the mail slot in the door. She went a little closer and said, "Is anyone there?"

"Sh!" said a voice from the mail slot.

Now Aurora was really surprised. She understood someone wanting to whisper through a mail slot; it was fun. She often called to Father through that very mail slot, but she had never called, "Sh!"

"Is anyone there?" she said, squatting down in front of the door.

"Yes, it's me." But the whisper was so low and the mail slot so narrow that hardly any sound came through.

"Who is me?" asked Aurora. She was getting impatient now.

"It's Daddy," said the voice a little louder. "Don't call out or say that I'm here."

"No," said Aurora. This was exciting. Daddy was out-side, talking to her, and she was the only one in the whole apartment who knew about it!

"There's something I want you to get for me," said Father.

"Yes," said Aurora. "Are you all right?"

"Oh yes," said Father.

At that moment Granny came into the hall. She was carrying some clothes that she wanted to wash in the bathroom. She saw Aurora crouching there. Granny stood quite still.

"We're all right, too," said Aurora, "but it won't be long before you come home again, Daddy, will it?"

"Poor child," said Granny, "she misses her father. Aurora, dear, do go into the kitchen and listen to Putten. She's practicing singing and it sounds so funny. And you can have an apple; I don't think you ate much breakfast."

"All right," said Aurora, jumping up. She shouted as loudly as she could, "I'm coming, Granny."

"I'm just going to fill the bath so that I can wash my clothes," said Granny.

"We can do our washing in the laundry room, too," said Aurora.

"I would rather do it up here," said Granny. "I'm not used to those machines."

"Daddy was the same way," said Aurora, "but he's over it now."

As soon as Granny went into the bathroom and turned the tap on, Aurora ran back to the front door and opened it.

Father stood there with his finger on his lips, smiling at her.

"Is there anybody in your room?" he whispered.

Aurora shook her head. She looked around carefully, opened the door of her room, and let him in. "If anyone comes you can hide in the closet," she said. "That's what Brit-Karen did that time we rescued her."

"Yes," said Father. "Now listen, Aurora. Go into my bedroom and see if you can find a white bow tie. Mommy bought it for me two weeks ago and I think I hung it on my closet door. And I need a book, too. It's on the bedside table."

"Why won't you say hello to Granny?" asked Aurora. Her voice sounded stern as she said this.

"Well, you know, today I have to read my paper to the examiners," said Father. "Granny gets very nervous when she thinks about it and that makes me nervous, too. I'd rather not talk to her until it's all over."

"But isn't Granny coming to listen to you?" asked Aurora. "She said she was."

"Yes, she is," said Father. "You and she are coming tomorrow and the next day."

"I see," said Aurora. "But not today?"

"No," said Father. "Granny isn't very strong, you know, and it doesn't do her any good to get worried. She knows I've only had two weeks to prepare the subject I'm going to speak about today, but I've had plenty of time for what I have to do tomorrow, so she's not so worried about that."

"I see," said Aurora. "I'll go and get the tie and the book."

Granny had filled the bathtub by now, and she put her head around the door of Aurora's room. "Why aren't you in the kitchen?" she asked.

"I just wanted to tell Little Puff something," said Aurora. This was true; she was sure that her doll Little Puff had been confused to hear Daddy in the hall after she had explained to him why Daddy was away.

Daddy had hidden in the closet, and luckily Granny

had no reason to look in there. She led Aurora into the kitchen and said to Putten, "Can we think of something nice to do today, so that Aurora doesn't miss her daddy?"

"We can go for a walk in the woods and see if there are any flowers yet," said Putten, "and we can hear the birds sing. I think they've just begun to know that spring is here."

"Oh yes, let's," said Aurora.

"Then I'll go into the bathroom and finish my washing before I go out," said Granny.

Putten went on trying to sing as she did the dishes, and Aurora slipped out and went into the bedroom.

There lay the book on the bedside table, and there were several ties hanging on the closet door, among them a white one.

Aurora just managed to reach it, but it was hanging over a string that caught it. She got the chair and carried it over to the closet as quickly as she could. Then she climbed up and easily was able to get the tie. Just as she was standing there with the tie in her hand, Granny came in.

"Why, my dear, what are you doing now?" she said.

"I'm tidying Daddy's ties," said Aurora.

"I'll rinse my clothes and then we'll be ready to go out," said Granny. "You can put your wraps on and wait outside."

"All right," said Aurora and ran into her own room.

"Well done, Aurora," said Father. "You're a smart girl. Do you have the book, too?"

"Yes, it's here under my apron," said Aurora proudly. "I'm going out. Can you wait a minute so that we can go together?"

"Yes, I can," said Father. "I have a fair amount of time to spare. We don't begin until one o'clock. Promise to think about me then."

"I promise," said Aurora. She put on her boots and her thick sweater and cap, and looked around to see if the coast was clear.

Granny was there again. "Are you ready?" she asked. "Have you wrapped up well?"

"Yes," said Aurora.

"Go outside and wait for us, then," said Granny. "But don't run off anywhere so that we can't find you."

"I won't," said Aurora. She went out and shut the door carefully behind her. Then she stood and waited.

She waited a long time. At last Father thought it was safe to come out. "I almost bumped into Socrates," he said. "Luckily he was so busy playing hide and seek with Putten that he didn't see me. Well, we'll tell Granny about it when it's all over."

"Not if she'd be upset," said Aurora. "She might be bothered that you didn't want to speak to her."

"We won't say anything, then," said Father. "Tomorrow and the next day she'll come and hear me in any case. I must be off now, Aurora. Remember to think about me at one o'clock."

Father ran down to the bus, and Aurora stood outside the building and waited. The others joined her a few minutes later, and they went for a nice walk in the woods. Aurora kept asking, "What's the time?"

When at last Granny answered, "It's one o'clock," Aurora thought hard about Father, and so everything went well for him.

9 · "Wish Me Luck!"

Gran had a busy day ahead of her. At that moment, she was leaving the house in the woods, and the mother of the eight children stood at the door and waved to her.

Gran was dressed up today in a beautiful white head scarf and her Sunday skirt. Her daughter wondered why. She knew Gran was going into town, but she didn't usually wear her best clothes for that. Perhaps she thought it was Sunday?

When Gran had walked a few steps, she turned around and called out, "Wish me luck and keep your fingers crossed for me!"

"What are you going to do?" said her daughter in alarm. "You're not ill, are you?"

"No, of course not," answered Gran, smiling, "I'm only joking," and she went quickly across the yard.

She waved when she reached the gate. Her daughter was used to Gran going into town. Usually she didn't think much about it, but there was something more to it today, she was sure of that. She almost went after Gran to find out what it was, but she told herself that she mustn't do that. If Gran wanted company, she would have said so.

Gran went to Tiriltoppen and then took the bus into town. When she got there, she went straight to the driving school. Her instructor was waiting for her.

"Hello, Gran," he said. "My word, you do look beautiful. That head scarf's enough to make you pass the test if your examiner's heart is in the right place."

"I hope it is," said Gran. "Mine is in my boots today."

"Now you and I are going for a little drive on our own first," said her instructor. "Just remember to take it nice and steady without being too slow, and keep a good lookout."

"Yes," said Gran. "Oh dear, I nearly went into that bus."

"No you didn't," said her instructor. "You put the brakes on in good time. I don't think the bus was afraid of you for a single moment."

"I wish you were the examiner," said Gran. "I'm used to your nonsense."

"That wouldn't do, Gran," said the instructor. "Just remember what we've talked about. You have it at your fingertips."

"Yes, at my fingertips," said Gran, "but it needs to be in my head, too."

"You're doing fine," said the instructor when they had driven around for a little while. "We'll pull up to the test center now. You sit here and wait for a minute or two, Gran, and a man will come and sit in the car beside you. Then you must drive as well as you can. I'll be in that cafe over there, waiting for you, but first I'll go in and find out whom you're going to drive with."

"All right," said Gran. She had told her daughter that she wasn't ill, but that was not true. She didn't feel like herself at all, and she couldn't remember a single word

she had learned. She got more and more scared. In a
little while she got out of the car. She couldn't bear to
sit there and wait for a strange man to come and tell her
whether she could drive or not. She would rather give
the whole thing up. She was walking down the sidewalk
when she felt a hand on her shoulder. "Why Gran, what's
the matter? The examiner's coming and he's a very nice
fellow. Just go and sit in the car."

"I can't," said Gran.

"Of course you can," said the driving instructor. "You
weren't running away, were you?"

"I don't know," said Gran, "but a little fresh air has
done me good."

She got into the car again. A man in a blue jacket
arrived, gave her the car key, and said, "My name's
Monsen."

"Mine's Mathea," said Gran.

"How many lessons have you taken?" asked Monsen.

"Two hundred and three with this one," answered Gran.

"Right, we'll have a little drive, then," said Monsen.

"Now I must remember everything that fellow told me," said Gran.

"What?" said Monsen.

"I'm just talking to myself," said Gran. "I must ask you about that before I start. Does it matter if I talk and think out loud while I'm driving?"

"Not a bit. Talk away," said Monsen. "Well, let's start and drive up there."

Gran didn't start. She turned the steering wheel and tested the hand brake. Then she put on the indicator and got out.

"What are you doing now?" asked Monsen.

"I'm just seeing that the car is in good order," said Gran. Then she switched on the ignition, gave a signal, looked carefully out of the window and in the mirror to make sure the way was clear, and drove away from the curb. It was a nice smooth start, with not so much as a tiny jerk.

"That was all right," said Gran, "but don't be too cocksure."

"Turn to the right up there," said Monsen.

"Yes, slow down, get into second gear, signal, and take the corner close to the curb," said Gran.

"We'll go left at the crossroads," said Monsen.

"Get into the middle of the road, signal, and make sure the way's clear on both sides because we're coming into a busier road here," said Gran.

"Now we'll go down that street," said Monsen.

"Very well, drive up to the pedestrian crossing, stop for the red light, check to see whether the oil pressure light is on. It shouldn't be. If it is, I must stop at once. The water in the radiator's all right—look at the nerve of that man, he's gone through on the yellow light! It's green now, keep up with the traffic, don't crawl. Oh dear, we're coming down into all that tieup in the center of town. You must put on the brakes if you get into trouble."

"We'll go up that street," said Monsen. "Which lane will you put yourself in?"

"I won't put myself anywhere," said Gran, "but I'll put the car into this lane. I have to stop for the people who are running for the bus. They shouldn't have to wait, they don't have much time. That's the way, now it's my turn. Look out, here I come with Mr. Examiner Monsen!"

"Well, we'll leave town now," said Monsen. When some time had passed and he hadn't said anything and Gran had kept on driving, he said, "Now we'll go up that steep hill on the right."

"That's steep all right, young man," said Gran. She drove up the hill in fine style, but just as she reached

121

the top there was a crossroads, and she stopped.

"We're hanging between heaven and earth now, but don't be afraid," she said. "We won't run backward. I had to stop, because a car might have come out at the very moment we got there."

"Splendid," said Monsen. "Now do a hill start."

"Right! The hand brake's on, I press the clutch down, get into first gear, listen to the buzz of the engine, and off we go."

They did so, and it was a very good hill start, but— another car came along just as Gran was getting up speed! This time Monsen had to brake hard with the extra brake he had in front of him.

"Oh dear, dear," said Gran, "it was going so well!"

"Yes," said Monsen. "You must have been thinking about that good hill start. All the same, you did well to stop when we came to the top of the hill. Drive on."

He hardly spoke again, just pointed where she was to go, and Gran, too, was silent after that little mishap. At last they were back where they had started.

"Right!" said Monsen. "Now let's see what you know about the engine." Hardly had he asked when Gran poured out the information. She reeled off everything she had learned for she had studied thoroughly.

When Monsen at last managed to stop her, he said, "Tell me, do you understand what you're saying?"

Gran looked at him with her honest eyes and answered, "No, not a word."

"Do you think you will do much driving?" asked Monsen.

"Oh no," said Gran, "I'm only going to borrow my son-in-law's truck and go over to Tiriltoppen and back to show him I can drive and give him a surprise."

"Is it a big truck?" asked Monsen.

"No, it's small," answered Gran.

"But what will you do otherwise? How will you manage to keep in practice?" said Monsen.

"I have a plan," said Gran, with a pleased look on her face.

Monsen sat and thought for a long time. "You really were good," he said. "I don't think we'll say any more about that little mistake, and you'll use your license sensibly, won't you?"

He filled in some papers and said, "Now go and get your license in that building over there."

"Thank you very much," said Gran, "that's very kind of you." She shook his hand and dropped a curtsey.

A little later, she held her license in her hand and trotted across to the cafe where her driving instructor was waiting. She looked very happy.

"Did you get it?" said the instructor. "I believe you did!"

"Yes," said Gran. "He said I was to be sensible. Now there's something I want to ask you. Would you mind driving with me as we've been doing, but only twice a month? I can't afford any more."

"But you don't need it now you've got your license," said the driving instructor.

"I enjoy it," said Gran. "When you're sitting beside me and have that extra brake of yours, I'm not nervous. Anyway I have to keep in practice. I haven't the heart to ask my son-in-law to lend me his truck more than once. It's the best friend he has."

"All right, Gran," said the driving instructor.

Gran was pleased. She was going home now and she had an exciting plan in her head.

10 · Surprise, Surprise!

When Gran came home that day with the driver's license in her skirt pocket, she had a mischievous look on her face. Before she reached the gate she stopped several times and took the license out and looked at it and put it back again.

Her daughter saw her from the window and called to her, "You're back. Is everything all right?"

"Oh yes, quite all right," said Gran.

"I've been worried," said her daughter. "You told me to keep my fingers crossed and wish you luck. What on earth was it all about?"

"You'll find out before the sun goes down," said Gran, "but don't say anything to the others yet."

"I can promise you that," said her daughter, "because I don't know myself what it is."

Only one person knew, and that was Morten. As soon as he came home from school, Gran called him into her bedroom. A lot of whispering went on, and when he came out again he looked as pleased as Gran had been, but he didn't say anything.

He and Gran were in an excited state right up until dinnertime. Soon the other children would be coming home and their father with his truck. . . . Gran stayed in her bedroom and waited.

"They're coming now!" said Morten.

"Right!" said Gran. She went into the kitchen and fiddled about with this and that.

Her son-in-law came in. He was tired, and glad to be home. Gran looked at him with twinkling eyes.

"Well, Gran, how are you?" he said, taking off his coat.

"Fine, thank you," said Gran, and hurried into Morten's bedroom. "I wanted to laugh so badly that I had to come in here," she said.

"We must go and have dinner now," said Morten. "I won't laugh, and you mustn't either."

He looked sternly at Gran, and she marched in to dinner with a straight face. All the same she couldn't help thinking about what she was going to do. Now and then she glanced at her son-in-law to see what kind of a mood he was in. He was in a teasing mood, and that was a good sign, for it meant he was in good spirits.

"What are you going to do now the winter's over?" he asked. "There won't be any more ski-jumping this year, will there?"

"Well, it will have to be athletics or football," answered Gran. She would have liked to say more, but she had decided to let him eat his meal in peace. She knew people as well as animals shouldn't be disturbed while they were eating.

But when he had finished his last spoonful of dessert and was starting to fill his pipe, Gran said, "Are you going to need the truck for the next hour?"

"The truck?" said her son-in-law. "No, I'm going to sit in the rocking chair and read the paper. Did you want me to drive you someplace?"

"Oh no," said Gran. "I just wondered whether Morten and I could sit in it for a little while."

"Of course you can," he said. "You two still enjoy having a game. They'll sit there and pretend they're driving," he said to the others. He went and got the key from his coat pocket.

"Can you open the door yourself, Gran?" he asked, "or do you want me to do it?"

"Don't bother," said Gran, "Morten and I will manage."

"Don't lose the key," said her son-in-law.

"We'll give it to you as soon as we come back," said Gran, "as soon as we get out of the truck, I mean."

"All right," he said. He had had a good meal, and he was tired and was looking forward to some peace and quiet. He sat down and looked at the paper. Now and then he glanced out of the window. His wife did the same. She meant to go upstairs and rest, for the older children did the washing up, but she stood there, looking out.

"Those two will never grow up," she said. "They take their games so seriously. Morten is opening the gate now so that they can pretend to drive out."

"Good!" grunted her husband. "Morten will have everything just so. He knows how things should be done."

They all had a good laugh about it. It took a minute for them to realize that the truck's engine was running. The truck drove out through the gate, stopped to let Morten get in, and went on.

Father stared, shut his eyes, and then stared again as

if he couldn't believe what he saw. There was his truck racing along the road. Then it simply disappeared into the trees.

"They're driving!" said Marte as if they couldn't all see that.

"Run!" said her father. "I can't, I ate too much, but you didn't. Run after them!"

Mads was already out of the door, and so was Mona, but Milly and Mina had to hunt for their shoes because they had kicked them off under the dinner table. Maren and Martin took things a little more calmly, but they went out as well.

Meanwhile the truck was going through the woods.

The road was rougher than the streets Gran was used to driving, but she knew it very well. She had walked along it every day for many years when she had to go to Tiril-toppen, and she knew where she could go fast and where she must drive very slowly.

"Are they coming?" she asked.

"I can't see anyone," said Morten. "Oh, now I think I can see Mads coming around that last bend. He's the best runner, so it's sure to be him."

"You do the talking if he catches up," said Gran. "I have to keep my eyes on the road and not let myself be distracted."

Mads overtook them when she had to drive extra slowly over some big roots that twisted across the road. He didn't have enough breath left to speak. Morten talked. Mads listened, gasped with surprise, and climbed on to the back of the truck.

At the next bump in the road, Mona and Marte managed to catch up with them. Mads signaled to them to jump up, and told them what Morten had told him. When they had come to the crossroads where they met the main road to Tiriltoppen, Gran waited for the others. "Up with you!" she said. Mona and Marte told Milly and Mina about Gran, and Milly and Mina told Maren and Martin, and so everybody knew.

"Gran's just going to drive round Tiriltoppen before she goes back," said Mads.

"Right!" said Martin. "We'll come, too."

Gran looked all around very carefully before she drove out on to the main road. They went up past the supermarket where she had met Aurora and her father and shown Aurora's father how to grind coffee, and on to Building Z. She drew up in front of the entrance and tooted cautiously. She looked up at the tenth floor, but it wasn't easy to see if there was anyone at home so high up. Well, you couldn't have everything you wanted, thought Gran, but she was luckier than she thought. A taxi stopped right in front of her. Out of it stepped a man in a dark suit and overcoat, and two ladies in hats and coats, and a little girl whom Gran recognized at once, for it was Aurora.

"Here I am," said Gran. They all looked at her. Aurora's granny opened her eyes wide and said, "My goodness, what a lovely head scarf you're wearing!" Aurora's mother came over and said, "It's not *you* driving?"

"Oh yes it is," said Father. "Congratulations, Gran!"

"Thank you," said Gran. "How are you getting on?"

"I've just come from reading my second paper to the examiners," said Father, "and I'm pleased so far. Tomorrow is the third and last day. Would you like to come and listen?"

"He's going to defend his thesis," said Aurora. She didn't rightly know what this meant, but she liked the sound of it.

131

"Oh, I couldn't do that," said Gran.

"Of course you could," said Father.

"I've never been to the university," said Gran.

"It's time you did come, then," said Father. "Just be there early and you can go into the old assembly hall with the others. But you'll have to go home without us, because we're going to have a dinner for those who've taken the exam. Aurora won't be there, of course. We think she would be bored sitting at the table so long."

"Perhaps Aurora can go home with Gran, then," said Mother.

"Yes, she can go with Gran and Nusse's mother," said Father. "Congratulations again, Gran!"

"I'll say the same to you tomorrow," said Gran.

"I'm glad you drove over here so that we could see you," said Father.

"So am I," said Gran.

She drove down the hill again and stopped in at the photographer's to show him her driver's license, because she had promised to tell him why she wanted her picture taken. When she had done this, she said, "Let's go home now so we don't scare your dad out of his wits."

At home, Dad was pacing up and down the yard and his wife was trying to calm him.

"Don't worry," she said. "Maybe Gran had a man hidden down there by the gate, and he was driving. Perhaps it's Henrik. There's sure to be some explanation, you'll see."

Shortly afterward, they heard the drone of an engine.

"I can see the truck now," said Dad. "It seems to be all right. Help, it's Gran driving! Is she crazy with all the children in the back? Look at them. They're shouting and waving as if they were out on a spree."

Gran drove in through the gate, turned around in the yard, drew up in the exact spot where the truck had been parked, put on the hand brake, and turned off the ignition. The children jumped out. Morten and Gran came last.

"Now I'd like an explanation," said her son-in-law.

Gran took her driver's license out and gave it to him.

"What?" he said. "Is this what you've been doing? If that doesn't beat the band! Have you really . . . ? Well, I'd never have believed it!"

"That's what I thought," said Gran, "and that's why I enjoyed doing it so much."

"It's wonderful," said her daughter. "Congratulations, Gran!"

"I only wanted to tease Dad a little," said Gran, "but don't be afraid that I'll take the truck out any more. It was just a joke. I'm going out with the driving instructor twice a month to keep in practice."

Her son-in-law was relieved to hear that, but he couldn't help taking a new look at her several times that evening.

"Tomorrow Edward has to defend his thesis as they call it, and I'm going to hear him do it," said Gran.

"Oh," said her son-in-law, "I'd like to hear him, too. He's an honorary member of the truck drivers' band, so it's almost my duty to be there. I'll ask Henrik to drive the truck tomorrow. You and I can go together, Gran."

Gran was pleased to hear this, for in fact she had been frightened at the idea of going to the university on her own. But when she went to bed that night, she thought more about the truck and her son-in-law than she did about the university. She chuckled happily to herself. Luckily there was only Stovepipe to hear her.

11 · All Together Again

Gran and her son-in-law got to the university a full half hour too early. He was wearing his best suit which he had purchased many years ago. It seemed to have gotten too small for him, and he hardly dared to breathe. But his chief worry was where in these three buildings they were to go. Aurora's father had told them, "In the old assembly hall," but they didn't know where it was. They had better wait until the others arrived.

"Let's pretend we're students," said Gran. "We'll walk around as if we belonged here." Plenty of others were doing the same. The courtyard was full of young people having a break from lectures. Many of them were sunning themselves on the big flight of steps outside the central building.

Gran's son-in-law didn't really succeed in feeling like

a student, but she herself felt certain she was studying something, only she wasn't quite sure what.

Luckily the others arrived when they had been walking about for a while. Aurora's hair was in braids today. She was wearing a coat and carrying a little handbag. All her attention was taken up with the handbag before she went into the building, but as soon as she came into the old assembly hall, all her thoughts were for Daddy. She had been here once before, but then Daddy had talked all the time and it was almost like being at home. She enjoyed listening to him even when he was hard to understand. Mommy had told her that today some other

people were going to speak and he was just going to defend himself. Aurora didn't like the sound of that very much.

She sat between Mother and Granny, and next to Granny were Gran and Father from the house in the woods, and Uncle Brande, and Nusse's mother.

There was no sign of Daddy. But after they had taken their places and were sitting there talking and looking up at the ceiling, a man in a sort of black robe came in, and behind him were three people in funny long black coats. One of them was Daddy.

"What's he wearing?" whispered Aurora.

"It's called a tailcoat," said Mother; she whispered something else in Aurora's ear, and Aurora nodded solemnly.

"Who's the man in the black robe?" asked Aurora.

"He's the dean," whispered Mother. "See what he's doing now."

He bowed politely to everyone and sat down at a table facing them. Daddy went up into a kind of pulpit, and one of the other men went up into another one.

"They've got two pulpits," whispered Gran. "Are they going to see which one of them can speak the fastest?"

The dean got up and said, "Edward Tege handed in his thesis on the childhood and youth of Socrates on the thirtieth of November last year." Then he said who had read it, but Aurora wasn't listening now, she was thinking about the day when Daddy had handed in his thesis. She and Mommy and Daddy had had dinner in a restaurant afterward. It was one of the nicest things they had ever done. She was sure it was much nicer than that candidates' dinner they talked so much about that she wasn't going to. When Aurora came back to the present again, the man in the other pulpit was speaking. He praised Daddy and said how intelligent he had been, and that he had handed in a fine piece of work which would open up new fields of research in this subject. His voice sounded dry and rather cracked, and Aurora thought that he ought to have had some hot black-currant syrup; that might have made it better. Otherwise he seemed all right, because he was nice to Daddy except at the very end when he began to find fault with some small details. But these weren't important, and he was satisfied, he said.

Aurora was pleased, too. Daddy had such a good answer for everything that she wasn't worried.

But then another man came, and he made Aurora angry from the start. In the first place he looked very self-important, and then he said that it seemed as if Daddy had been short of time, for there were several places where he might have put commas.

He said a whole lot of other things, too. He said something nice here and there, but he didn't sound at all pleased and seemed to be insulting Daddy to his face. Aurora hardly dared to look at Daddy. He must be feeling awful. Now he was blowing his nose. What if he was crying and didn't want anyone to see? She caught at Mother's arm. "Tell that man he mustn't talk like that," she said.

"It's all right, Aurora," said Mother. "Daddy will defend himself afterward."

"Can't you defend him?" whispered Aurora. "You're a lawyer." Mother had often told her how she had defended someone who had done wrong when she was in court.

"Don't worry," whispered Mother, "and stop talking."

Aurora stared at the floor. Not for anything in the world would she look at that horrible man. She didn't want to look at Daddy either, in case he thought things weren't going too well.

But when the man had finished, Daddy was as cheerful as ever, and was so ready with his answers and so amusing that he made a lot of people smile. Finally the dean said something nice and then it was all over, for people got up, and they all seemed to know Daddy and went over to shake hands with him.

Mother took Aurora over to him, too, and Father bent down and gave her a good hug, but then he said, "Now you must come and meet my opponents, Aurora," and led her up to the two men who had spoken against him. Aurora offered her hand to the first one, but when she came to the other one she hid her hands behind her back.

"Why, Aurora, aren't you going to shake hands nicely?" said Father.

"No," said Aurora, "he said a lot of mean things. Can *you* look after babies?" she said, glaring at his opponent. "Could *you* have taken care of Socrates, and washed diapers, and looked after me, and cooked, and take a degree as well?"

The man looked astounded and gazed at her helplessly. Father was horrified.

"Oh, Aurora!" he said.

"I thought he was very unkind," whispered Aurora. But then the man got his voice back, and he smiled kindly at Aurora and said, "I envy your daddy for having such a brave daughter to defend him."

"You see," said Father, "he had to stand up there and find a lot of things to criticize, otherwise there wouldn't have been any reason for me to defend myself."

"Oh," said Aurora, "I'll shake hands with him, then."

"That's a good girl," said Father. "Now you must go home with Gran and Nusse's mother."

"Have a nice dinner," said Aurora solemnly, and left. She was a little sad that Mother and Father and Granny were staying behind and she was going, but she soon forgot about it, because on the bus going home Gran and the father of the eight children in the woods and Nusse's mother talked about Daddy the whole time. Aurora swelled with pride.

"How clever he was!" said Gran.

"He spoke up for himself so well!" said Nusse's mother. "Nobody got the better of him, and he looked so handsome in those clothes."

"Yes, he ought to wear them always," said Gran.

"He can't," said Aurora, "Mommy whispered to me that he rented them, but the white bow tie was his own."

"Oh, I see," said Gran.

They went as far as Tiriltoppen together. Then Gran and her son-in-law went home to the house in the woods, and Nusse's mother took Aurora up to Socrates and Putten. At home there were flowers everywhere that people had sent to Father. Putten hadn't been able to find enough vases, and so the bathtub looked like a flowerbed. She had made pancakes, too. Aurora felt sure that their dinner was better than the one Mother and Father were having.

Next morning, when Aurora woke up, Father was sleeping in the living room. He had come home again. That was the first nice thing that happened that day. There were others. More flowers arrived for Father, and letters, too. Granny was so proud of her son that she had to read all the letters aloud to the rest of them.

Socrates ran about and jumped up and down and said, "Daddy, Daddy back, Daddy not under chair."

"It's good to be home again!" said Father, looking at Aurora and Socrates. "I'm glad it's all over. I can't bear to be away from you."

"You'll have to get used to it, though," said Granny. "You'll be looking for a permanent job now you've finished your doctorate."

"Marie has a permanent job," said Father. "I think I may do some more research at home and some writing. Besides, I'd like to study the ancient Egyptians, and of course I want to take up the piano again."

"Now you're only joking, Edward," said Granny. "You've always been such a tease."

There was a ring at the door. It was Nusse, who had brought a cake and some flowers. "The cake's from

Mommy and the flowers are from me," she said. "I saved up for them myself. Can you soon begin to give me piano lessons again?"

"Yes, we'll start next week," said Father.

Aurora stole a glance at him.

"You too, Aurora," he said.

Aurora was so happy that she had to go and tell Little Puff.

"Do you want to go out and play?" said Nusse after a while.

"Yes," said Aurora—for now Daddy was at home again and she felt she could go out and play with Nusse and Brit-Karen and all the children in Building Z, and all the children of Tiriltoppen, and all the children in the world, if she liked.